'There you are.' Nic said the first thing that came to mind. 'I've been looking everywhere for you.'

Charlotte blinked. One moment she was trying desperately to deny her identity to the press, the next she was being swept against some dark-shirted stranger with abs of steel who seemed to think she was someone else.

Large hands held her in place, and a deep voice against her cheek murmured, 'Trust me and play along.'

For an instant a whole other 'play along' scenario scorched the back of her eyeballs as his lips teased and toyed with hers. She was vaguely aware of the voices around them blurring into one meaningless hum. This guy could *kiss*. Somewhere an inner voice warned her that she didn't know him…but instead of easing away, as she should be doing, she *kissed him back*.

D1143919

Anne Oliver was born in Adelaide, South Australia, and with its beautiful hills, beaches and easy lifestyle, she's never left.

An avid reader of romance, Anne began creating her own paranormal and time travel adventures in 1998 before turning to contemporary romance. Then it happened—she was accepted by Harlequin Mills and Boon for their Modern Heat series in December 2005. Almost as exciting; her first two published novels won the Romance Writers of Australia's Romantic Book of the Year for 2007 and 2008. So after nearly thirty years of yard duties and staff meetings, she gave up teaching to do what she loves most—writing full time.

Other interests include animal welfare and conservation, quilting, astronomy, all things Scottish, and eating anything she doesn't have to cook. She's traveled to Papua/New Guinea, the west coast of America, Hong Kong, Malaysia, the UK and Holland.

Sharing her characters' journeys with readers all over the world is a privilege and a dream come true.

You can visit her website at www.anne-oliver.com

Recent titles by the same author:

THE MORNING AFTER THE WEDDING BEFORE
THERE'S SOMETHING ABOUT A REBEL
HER NOT-SO-SECRET DIARY

THE PRICE OF FAME

BY
ANNE OLIVER

First published in Great Britain 2012
by Mills & Boon, an imprint of Harlequin (UK) Limited.
Harlequin (UK) Limited, Eton House, 18-24 Paradise Road,
Richmond, Surrey TW9 1SR

© Anne Oliver 2012

ISBN: 978 0 263 89331 1

Harlequin (UK) policy is to use papers that are natural, renewable and recyclable products and made from wood grown in sustainable forests. The logging and manufacturing process conform to the legal environmental regulations of the country of origin.

Printed and bound in Spain
by Blackprint CPI, Barcelona

THE PRICE
OF FAME

CHAPTER ONE

NIC RUSSO always planned for contingencies. The volcanic ash cloud from Chile sweeping across southern Australia had already disrupted air travel and any moment all flights out of Melbourne's Tullamarine would be grounded.

His instincts were always spot on and Nic didn't intend being one of those passengers caught up in the chaos.

In line at the airline's business check-in, he speed-dialled Reception at the airport hotel, heard Kerry's familiar, but somewhat distracted voice on the other end and smiled. 'Hey, babe. It's Nic.'

'Nic, hi.'

'How's it going there?'

'Hectic.'

'I bet. Reckon I'm going to need that reservation after all.'

'You're not the only one. There's a waiting list a mile long.'

'Ah, but they don't know the receptionist like I do.' He grinned. 'Connections, Kerry babe.'

'Are everything. Right.' He could hear the clatter of her fingers flying over her keyboard. 'So…that's for one guest?'

'Depends…' He deepened his voice and drawled, 'What time do you get off?'

The muffled cough was laced with friendly amusement. 'You're incorrigible, Nic.'

'So you keep telling me.' He could envision the humour in her eyes and knew Kerry and her partner, Steve, would have a laugh over it later tonight. 'If I'm still grounded when you get off, do you want to come by for a thank-you drink?'

While he talked, his attention was drawn to the slim brunette in line ahead of him. She'd been a passenger on his flight from Adelaide earlier in the day. He'd noticed her perfume then and he noticed it now—French and expensive but cool and light and refreshing.

Was it only her perfume that captured his interest? Neat and conservative weren't his type but there was…something about her. Something timeless.

The notion tickled him for a moment. But only for a moment, because Nic didn't do that nostalgic sentimental nonsense where women were concerned. In fact, he didn't do sentimental, period.

But it was exactly how she made him feel, and that was weird. He could imagine standing behind her just this way on the edge of a still lake and watching the stars come out. Flicking aside her single strand of pearls and the glossy hair that had escaped its knot and putting his mouth right there, on that slender neck—

'I'd love to catch up,' he heard Kerry say, jolting him back to the noisy, overcrowded terminal, 'but at this point with everything so uncertain I don't know how long my shift's going to be.'

'No worries. You're busy; I'll let you get on with it. Maybe I'll see you shortly. *Ciao*.'

He disconnected, his eyes still focused on the back of the woman's neck. Shaking away the odd feeling she'd invoked, he studied her from a purely objective viewpoint.

Who wore pearls these days? Unless she'd dressed for a royal garden party.

His gaze wandered over her shoulders, covered in a slippery-looking fade-into-the-background jacket, then down to a matching knee-length skirt over a well-rounded, caressable bottom. A sexy little handful. Warmth flooded his palm—and other places. He could do a tea party if it meant taking her home after...

Tea party? Pearls? Hell, if that turned him on, his libido needed some serious attention. It had been a dry couple of months, after all.

She'd been in the aisle seat one row back and across from him, plugged into her music player, eyes glued shut every time he looked, fingers stiff on her lap. No rings on her left hand, he'd noticed, but a heavy chunk of bling on her right. Maybe she suffered from the same affliction he did? But the suffocatingly claustrophobic effect of being hermetically sealed in a flying tin can was a tedious necessity in his life.

Whatever the reason for her tension, she'd been an intriguing distraction. Her apparent lack of interest had given him the opportunity to glance back every so often and wonder whether that peach-glossed mouth would taste as luscious as it looked. How she'd respond if he put his theory to the test. The expression he'd see if she opened those eyes and saw him watching.

He grinned to himself—yeah, that was more like him. The excitement of the chase, the inevitable conquest. And temporary. None of that timeless sentimental rubbish.

He shuffled forward with the line.

So she was also travelling to Fiji and flying Tabua Class. She didn't look like a businesswoman; not in that insipid suit that whimpered 'don't look at me', but she didn't look like a tourist either. Maybe she'd have the seat next to him and he could spend the next few hours finding out what colour her eyes were and whether or not a hot-blooded woman lay beneath that drab, conservative exterior.

Assuming the aircraft got off the ground.

She stepped up to the counter and slid a high-end brand-name suitcase onto the conveyor. A moment later, he watched her walk away, those mystery eyes hidden behind a pair of supersized sunglasses. A celebrity or a wealthy socialite? he wondered, swinging his own travel-battered bag onto the conveyor and reaching for his documents. Whoever she was, he didn't recognise her.

He proceeded to Immigration and Customs, unable to keep his eyes off the enticing sway of her backside a few metres ahead. *Forget it, Nic, she's not your type, remember?* Except his body didn't want to listen. So he deliberately stopped, shrugged off his jacket and stowed it in his cabin bag and studied the departures board a moment. He was supposed to be using the flight to brainstorm the ins and outs for his current computer game, not lusting after some unknown woman. Who wasn't his type.

He'd not gone far when he caught sight of her again amongst the milling crowd. And all casual, carnal thoughts vanished. A reporter he recognised from one of the local gossip rags stood in her way. She was shaking her head and attempting to move on, but the guy, easily twice her size, was blocking her progress, shadowing her steps as he towered over her. Intimidating her.

Nic's gut tightened reflexively as his own childhood images charged back. And now, as then, not a single person intervened or came to her assistance. No one cared, no one wanted to get involved.

No way. He swung his cabin bag over his shoulder and moved fast, the hand on the strap jammed into a fist. No way would he stand by and allow the bully to get away with it.

'Leave me alone,' he heard her say as he neared. She was standing her ground, one palm thrust in front of her, then she shook her head again, trying—and failing—to pass. 'I've already told you, you've mistaken me for some-one el—'

'There you are.' Nic said the first thing that came to mind. 'I've been looking everywhere for you.' Keeping his hands easy and non-threatening, he touched her rigid shoulders and turned her to face him.

Beneath her flawless complexion she looked pale and stunningly fragile, a vanilla rose facing the dawn of sum-mer's first heatwave. Up close her skin-warmed perfume was even more sensuous. Damn, what were her eyes say-ing behind that sunglass shield?

He didn't take his eyes off her face, willing her to give him a chance to show he meant no harm, and said, 'Clear off, mate, she already told you, you've got the wrong woman.'

Charlotte blinked. One moment she was trying desperately to deny her identity, the next, she was being swept against some dark-shirted stranger with abs of steel who seemed to think she was someone else.

Large hands held her in place and a deep voice against her cheek murmured, 'Trust me and play along.'

She froze, her already hammering heart tripping against her ribs, her insides trembling. She couldn't have freed herself anyway; she was gripping the handle of her cabin wheel-bag in one hand, her documents and handbag in the other, and his arms were like prison bars. Well, not quite, because they were big and warm and somehow protective rather than restrictive.

As if he knew she'd had a recent run-in with the press and was desperate to avoid another. But he didn't appear to recognise her so she grabbed the lifeline he seemed to be offering with a vengeance, met his eyes and forced her lips into a smile. 'And here I am... *Honey Pie*.'

His brows lifted a fraction at that, then, nodding once, he returned a co-conspiratorial grin, his hands sliding off her shoulders and down her back.

And before she could draw another breath, his mouth touched hers. Tender yet firm but not hard and controlling. *Trust me and play along.* His words played back to her in that wholly masculine rumble that still echoed in her breasts, making them swell and throb with a tantalising heat.

For an instant, a whole other 'play along' scenario scorched the backs of her eyeballs as his lips teased and toyed with hers. She was vaguely aware of the voices around them blurring into one meaningless hum. This guy could *kiss*. Somewhere an inner voice warned her that she didn't know him...except instead of easing away as she should be doing, she *kissed him back*.

He pulled her closer, dived deeper and took complete possession. Of her mouth, her senses, her...everything. It was like falling and flying at the same time. She'd never experienced anything like it. Somewhere in the dim distance she was aware of an announcement over the PA system but the part of her brain that processed rational thought had already shut down.

She could feel his hands sliding lower, fingers playing over her spine and settling on her hips, beneath the hem of her jacket and against her skirt so that she could feel every pressure point his fingers made through the thin silk. His warmth soaked clear through her underwear to shimmer on her skin, coarse denim rasped against her skirt as his thighs came into contact with hers.

A moan rose up her throat. He was hard as rock. Everywhere. It made her feel soft and feminine and totally boneless and she found herself sagging against him.

He changed the angle of the kiss, bumping her glasses with his cheek or nose and tilting them sideways. She felt the pressure of his lips lessen and wanted to cling a moment longer—wanted *more*, *deeper*, *hotter*—but he lifted his head and straightened the glasses on her face and grinned. An intimate we're-sharing-a-secret kind of grin. 'Missed you too, *babe*.'

'Uh-huh.' She felt as if she were waking from a trance. She realised she'd stopped breathing and drew in some much-needed air. A whiff of some unfamiliar spicy fragrance teased her nostrils. The intimacy of the moment lessened, but her pulse was still stammering, colour and commotion and movement swirling all around her as she stared up at him.

His eyes...the deepest darkest brown, she noticed now. Mesmerising, compelling. The kind of eyes you could lose yourself in and never find your way back... She tightened her slippery grip on her belongings. 'I—'

He touched a long tanned finger to her lips, glanced over her shoulder and gave her a look alerting her that the media pest was still watching, then said, 'We'd better get moving—pandemonium's about to break out.' Curling a hand around her upper arm, he began to guide her towards the exit.

'Hang on!' She stopped. This was suddenly moving way too fast. 'Where are you taking me? What is *going on*?'

'Shh.' His warm breath tickled her ear, making her toes curl inside her shoes. 'Didn't you hear the announcement?' A flicker of barely there humour crossed his gaze—as if he knew she hadn't. 'All flights are grounded until tomorrow morning at the earliest.' Tightening his grip, but not so much that it felt threatening or uncomfortable, he propelled her forward. 'So we're going to the airport hotel.'

Of course she hadn't heard any announcement. She'd been otherwise occupied. Blind and deaf and mute to everything but him. His hands resting with familiar ease on her waist, his lips moving expertly and intimately over hers as if they were long-term lovers...

She didn't even know his name.

She jerked to a halt as warmth flooded into her cheeks. 'Wait. Just wait. I don't—'

'You'd rather stay here and take your chances?' He glanced at her, one eyebrow raised, his dark eyes assessing.

No. Definitely not. Wise or foolish, she'd take her chances with Mr Expert Kisser.

He tugged on her hand, giving her no further time to consider her options. 'Your stalker's following us—don't look back.'

A shiver ran down her spine as she struggled to keep up. Difficult when her knees still felt like clotted cream. 'How do you know?'

'I know how the guy's mind works.' They were approaching the terminal's glass doors, being swept along with the tide of noise and people. 'He's watching to see if our impromptu display of affection continues. Waiting for us to slip up.'

'But my luggage...'

'Has been checked through. You'll have to make do with what you've got.'

They walked out into a dull winter's late afternoon. Passengers who hadn't heard the news were still arriving, others were diving into taxis as fast as they pulled into the kerb and disgorged their load.

She accompanied him towards the sky bridge that led to the multi-storey car park and hotel. 'I'm sure we convinced him,' she murmured, yanking her wheel-bag up over the kerb and onto a strip of grass. Heavens, this guy had convinced *her*—introverted scene-avoider, Charlotte Dumont. And in more ways than one.

'Convincing, you reckon?' He stopped, looked down at her, lips curved into that devastatingly intimate-secret grin again. His eyes were twinkling. Or maybe it was just the sun momentarily peeking out from behind the clouds. 'I think we should give it another try,' he said. 'To be absolutely certain.' Before she knew what he was about to do, he slipped the glasses off her face. 'Ah,' he murmured.

She jerked her chin up, daring herself to meet his gaze. 'You were expecting brilliant blue or moss green? Violet maybe? I appreciate your help,' she hurried on before he could pay her some smoothly delivered yet empty compliment she didn't want to hear. She bent to unzip the side pocket of her bag, slid her documents inside, then straightened. 'Really. Thank you. But was all that...' she waved a hand, trying to find the right words to express the almost orgasmic experience and failing '...necessary?'

Orgasmic? One kiss? Oh, she so needed to get a life. A *new* life. And wasn't that why she was taking this trip? Time away to ponder her future and decide what she wanted to do? Which could, just maybe, include spicing up her non-existent sex life?

'Absolutely it was necessary.' His eyes remained on hers as he dumped his cabin bag at his feet. 'Subtleties are lost on guys like him.'

'Okay.' She nodded. 'Right. But I don't think we need to repeat the performance.'

He glanced towards the terminal. 'Think again, *babe*.'

'Oh, no.' She didn't look, snatching at her glasses instead, but he shook his head, holding them out of her reach. He stood so close she could feel his heat all down the front of her body.

He caressed the side of her face with his thumb. 'He can't be sure you're who he thinks you are—he's too far away to see the colour of your eyes. And that's his loss because they're enchanting.'

Oh, please. Flynn had been a smooth-talking charmer too. 'They're *grey*.' She resisted reaching for her glasses again because that was exactly what he was expecting her to do.

'Is there a reason you hide them behind sunglasses?' he asked, studying her closely. Curiously.

No way was she spilling her family history. 'I woke up with a headache, if you really want to know.'

'Sorry to hear that. How is it now?'

'Better. Shall we get this over with, then?'

One eyebrow rose. 'You liked it well enough a moment ago.'

And she had. She sure had.

He touched her face again. 'You should make the moves this time. Persuade him you're hopelessly besotted with me.'

A stiff breeze ruffled his hair. Black hair too long to call tidy, dark brows and olive skin that told her he was of Mediterranean descent. He had a square masculine jaw and prominent cheekbones. Lines crinkled at the corners of his eyes, as if he enjoyed life in the outdoors. His sensuous mouth curved easily and told her he also enjoyed more than a little indoors activity.

Hopelessly besotted? How could she be? She'd never laid eyes on him before. And yet she couldn't have said it better herself. And that should worry her because she wasn't going to be lured and seduced by another man's suave talk and good looks ever again. A man who undoubtedly knew exactly what he was doing, and did it often and well. 'I don't even know your name...'

Amusement touched his lips. 'It's Nic. Yours?'

She shook her head, rolled her lips together, then said, 'I should tell you he didn't have the wrong woman and he's probably an expert lip-reader.'

His gaze immediately dropped to her mouth and those dreamy brown eyes darkened. 'All the more important to head him off, then, don't you think? Kiss me.'

His husky demand stroked her skin and she rubbed her jacket and the goose-bumps that sprang out on her arms beneath her sleeves. 'I...' *Don't kiss men I don't know.* Except she already had.

'Say my name first if it makes you more comfortable.'

As if he knew her concerns. 'Nic.' She liked the way it sounded on her tongue. She liked the fact that he was doing his best to put her at ease. That he'd just saved her from public humiliation. That he was possibly the most stunning-looking guy she'd ever laid lips on. 'Nicholas...?'

'Dominic.'

'Dominic.' Reaching out, not quite able to look him in the eye, she placed a tentative palm on his chest. His shirt felt warm and smooth against her fingertips. Hard muscle shifted beneath her hand— Her fingers jerked away instinctively.

But what had Flynn said when he'd ended their engagement? She wasn't outgoing enough, not glamorous enough, not confident enough to be any aspiring politician's wife. That after twenty-four years as the daughter of a socially distinguished couple, she should be used to being in the public eye.

Since then she'd made a decision to work on her shortcomings. Hence this trip. To relax, regroup and refocus on the new direction her life had taken. To work on improving her confidence. She so wanted to prove her ex wrong. Then she could move on. And hadn't she already proved with that horrible reporter that she could be confident when it counted?

'Hey,' he murmured, catching her hand and putting it back against his shirt. 'Just shut your eyes and go with it. If it helps, pretend I'm someone else.'

No way. If she was going to do this, she was going to enjoy it, and that meant giving him her full attention. Her new life's direction could afford a little side-trip along the way. Then she'd book herself a room for what was left of today and this evening. She wouldn't have to see him again—all flights out of Melbourne did *not* go through Fiji.

So she took a deep breath, then boldly moved her hand over his shirt, taking her time, enjoying the sensation as she let herself relax and acquainted herself with the rugged unfamiliar terrain. Her other hand joined in—there was…so much of him. This excursion could take hours.

Disgruntled passengers trailing baggage and bad language flowed around them, as if they were an island in a flood-swollen river. Heavy exhaust fumes and the odour of jet fuel from aircraft not going anywhere clogged the air but all she could smell was Nic's spicy fragrance and warm masculine skin.

'Nic.' She met his direct gaze and said, 'Is there some woman out there somewhere who's going to want to scratch my eyes out?'

His lips curved boyishly. 'I could ask the same of you,' he said. 'It's a no from me.'

Charmed against her will—and wickedly turned on by that sexy mouth—she smiled back. 'And it's a no from me.'

'So no more procrastinating.'

She moistened her dry still-tingly lips. 'Is he still watching, do you think?'

That kiss-me-I'm-gorgeous smile continued playing around his mouth as he toyed with the button on her jacket, knuckles grazing her chest, eyes locked on hers. 'Does it matter?'

Her nipples tightened beneath his barely there touch and the corner of her mouth curved up. 'No.' Not one iota. Right now it *so* didn't matter. Give Stalker Man something to gawk at and enjoy herself at the same time, right? Meanwhile, the pest would get the message, find someone else to harass and she'd be free to reclaim her anonymity. All perfectly public and safe.

'Nic.' She rose up on tiptoe and planted her lips on his. *Not* tentatively this time. Winding her arms around his neck, fingers playing with the tips of his silky hair, surprised and amazed that she could let herself and her inhibitions fly away so easily.

Nic's wasn't the smooth, close-shaven jaw she was accustomed to and the unfamiliar masculine texture tickled her chin, sending reverberations all through her body. Which hadn't happened in a really long time.

Her mouth softened and parted without any help on her part. He swallowed her sigh and quickly took the lead, his tongue sliding against hers as he shifted closer, his hands sliding over her bottom, tucking her against him. Outrageously intimate and a long way from publicly acceptable.

She didn't know and she didn't care how long they stood there, locked together until she heard a man mutter, 'Get a room,' as he trudged by.

Nic broke away; his head came up. 'Sounds like good advice.' His voice sounded a little hoarse and husky. He slid her glasses back on her face, then picked up his bag, hefted it onto his shoulder. 'Let's go.'

'Wait...'

He glanced back at her and Charlotte saw that his eyes had changed. Not just amused now, but...surprised? As if she wasn't what he'd expected. And hungry, as if he'd like to devour her at the first opportunity. A delicious little shiver shimmied down her spine.

She looked about at the passengers already swarming over the sky bridge towards the hotel. A curious mix of disappointment and relief threaded through her system. 'Looks like we might already be too late.'

Grinning, he caught her hand. 'Then it's lucky I booked a room earlier.'

CHAPTER TWO

LUCKY for *him*, she decided when they arrived in the congested lobby. Because now she thought about it—rationally—no way was she going with him to his room, no matter how expert a kisser he was. She'd filled her quota of daring, uncharacteristic behaviour for…oh, the next ten years or so.

'Wait here,' he told her as they entered. And as if the crowd parted for him, he made his way to the desk and spoke to one of the busy staff. But Charlotte shuffled to the end of the queue. There had to be *something* still available.

He returned moments later holding a couple of swipe cards. 'Okay, we're set.'

She shook her head. 'Thanks for everything, but I want to book my own room.'

Quirking an eyebrow, he grinned. 'You don't trust me after all we've shared?'

And that was the thing, wasn't it? She'd shared *all that* with a stranger. 'So why *did* you kiss me?' she murmured as the crowd milled around them.

He grinned. 'You can ask me that when you called me *honey pie*?'

There was that. 'You could've just stopped at "get lost"…'

His grin vanished. 'I don't like bullies.' He shrugged but she saw the tension in his shoulders. 'I just reacted.'

And she knew right then that he'd had firsthand experience with harassment. Something in his own past had triggered his Good Samaritan act. 'Thank you,' she said quietly.

'If I—'

'Please don't apologise.' *I enjoyed every memorable mind-numbing second.*

'Why would I apologise?' The grin was back. 'I'm not the least bit sorry. Are you?'

Not at all. But it was over. 'Thanks for your help but I still want to get my own room.'

'With this crowd?' He shook his head. 'There's someone I want you to meet.' He guided her to the business side of the desk, a light hand at her back. 'Kerry, this is...?'

'Charlotte.'

'Charlotte.' He said her name like a caress, his eyes lingering on hers as he said, 'Is there anything you can do for my friend here?'

Kerry, an attractive blonde with cornflower-blue eyes, barely looked up, her fingers busy on her keyboard. 'Sorry, Charlotte, we're fully booked. But Nic spoke with me and we're happy for you to share at no extra cost.'

Their earlier performance played in front of Charlotte's eyes like some hot romance movie. A public kiss was one thing, sharing a room with a guy she knew next to nothing about was something else, no matter how chivalrous he seemed. 'It's okay.' She tightened the grip on her bag and prepared for a long evening ahead. 'I'll buy a book or magazine and find somewhere else to wait.'

Kerry flicked Nic a look, then motioned Charlotte aside. 'My partner, Steve, and I have known Nic for years. He's an okay guy. You've got the chance to spend the next twelve hours or so in comfort; I'd take it if I were you.'

Charlotte nodded. 'Thanks, anyway.'

'Your decision.' Kerry inclined her head. 'Excuse me...'
She was already moving away to deal with a woman who
had one hysterical child attached to her leg.

'Look, you take the room.' Nic pushed a swipe card into
her hand. 'I'll use the gym, catch up on some work at the
business centre, then chill out in the terminal. I'll let you
know when they're flying again.'

'Oh, no. That's very generous but I can't accept.' It just
wouldn't be right. '*I'll* wait in the terminal.'

He frowned towards the lobby's entrance. 'What if our
friend turns up again? The jerk's persistent enough. And
sneaky enough.'

Charlotte's skin crawled and she couldn't help glancing
towards the crowded entrance. 'Then I'll just come clean
with him and maybe he'll leave me alone. About that... I
should probably explain...'

'But you don't want to. And that's okay, I don't need to
know your business. Here's what we'll do.' He curled his
hands around her upper arms. 'We'll check into the room
together, then I'll park my stuff and leave you to it. Okay?'

There was an openness and honesty in those dark eyes.
So attractive, so alluring. And something she hadn't seen
since that last time her father had kissed her goodbye
and called her his princess. Right before her family had
climbed aboard the doomed helicopter...

Her father had been the one man she'd always been able
to count on. To trust. Somehow she imagined Dad would
approve of Nic. That he'd tell her she could trust him too.

She nodded once, but for the life of her she couldn't
make her voice work.

'Right, then, that's settled.' He took charge of her bag
and they walked towards the elevators.

They didn't speak in the crowded lift. Nor as they
walked down the dim, thickly silent corridor to their room.

Nic swiped his card in the slot, motioned her through, then followed with their hand luggage.

The clouds had rolled away, leaving a hard blue sky. Blinding late afternoon sunshine flooded in, reflecting off the distant tarmac where scores of stranded aircraft waited for the ash cloud to lift. Her temples throbbed with the light's intensity and the memory of a dull headache from earlier echoed at the back of her skull. She drew the heavy drapes closed. And with the imprint of their kiss still hot on her lips, she realised immediately how her action might be misconstrued.

The room was plunged into semi-darkness and the intimacy wasn't lost on Nic. Shadows softened Charlotte's features but he could see the puckered brow, the tense stance as her fingers twisted on the edge of the curtain. She wasn't comfortable with the situation.

Nor was he, but for entirely different reasons. He'd been in a painful state of arousal since he'd discovered she tasted even more luscious than he'd imagined—and he'd imagined quite a lot. He indicated the closed drapes. 'Headache still bothering you? Do you want to take a nap?' *Do you want me to join you?*

'No to both, but thank you.' Something flashed across her eyes, as if she shared his let's-get-naked thoughts. But maybe her tension wasn't the anticipation he hoped for because she only said, 'I might watch TV awhile. If that's okay with you?'

'Fine. Make yourself comfortable. I'm going for a run.'

Without looking at her, he yanked a pair of shorts, a T-shirt and running shoes out of his backpack and went to the bathroom to change. He needed to release some of his own tension and a dose of cold Melbourne air would cool his blood. The colder the better.

He splashed water on his face and checked himself out

in the mirror. A smear of her lip gloss glistened on his lips. He smiled at his reflection as he rubbed it away. Now he knew. Ms Neat and Conservative on the outside wasn't so conservative on the inside. Perhaps they could—

He shook the images away, ran his fingers through his hair and glared at himself. He'd offered her refuge. And that changed the rules. It was entirely her call if she wanted to take it further. Still… He shook his head and turned away from the mirror. Absolutely not.

He considered taking a cold shower but decided against it. Getting naked and knowing she was probably spread out on that bed watching TV wasn't going to do him any favours.

When he returned from the bathroom, she was standing right where he'd left her. The big screen was still blank, the room was still silent. But the atmosphere had changed. Her fragrance and the scent of her skin smelled sharper, warmer. Damper. She must have turned up the thermostat on the air conditioning because it felt a damn sight hotter in here than it had moments ago.

Her eyes skimmed down his body and he felt as though a thousand fiery pinpricks had blistered every square centimetre of skin.

Then she snatched up the TV remote. Put it down. Drew in a sharp breath as if she'd come to a decision and was wondering whether to let him in on it.

'Everything all right?'

'Look, I don't want to kick you out of your room. Please. Stay. I'm fine with it.' Her gaze shifted to the double bed, then snapped back to him and he swore the air around them crackled. 'In fact, I'd feel a lot better if you stayed.'

Yeah? He smiled—so would he. 'Okay…' That glint in her eyes… Hot. Wary too, but definitely hot. His whole body tightened, stiffened, and a bead of sweat trickled down his back. In a deliberately casual move, he laid his discarded clothes on the back of the office chair at the desk. 'So what's your real name? Or aren't we going to get into all that?'

'I told you, it's Charlotte.' She slid her palms down her skirt as if they were sticky. 'But no surnames, no talking about ourselves and swapping life histories. We'll be gone tomorrow.'

His thoughts precisely. So…she wanted to play… Nothing personal, nothing complicated. One night. This had to be his lucky day. The surprise of it, and of her, was like a mid-winter's heatwave. 'Fine by me.'

'I'm going to take a shower now,' she said, suddenly and randomly, as if plucking the words from the increasingly sultry atmosphere. 'Alone.' She moved to her bag, unzipped it, then tossed him an I-mean-it look over her shoulder. 'I'll see you shortly.'

'Right.' So she wanted time to get ready; he didn't mind waiting. 'I'm off for that run, then. When I get back…' at the door, he looked her over the way she'd looked at him—though he might have lingered a tad longer '…we'll see how we get along.'

He took the stairs down to the lobby two at a time. He saw Kerry amidst the carnage, sticking a sign on the door advising alternative accommodation, and stopped.

'Is your friend okay?' she said, giving him a quick glance as she smoothed the sign in place.

'She is.'

She shook her head on her way back to the desk. 'And by that glazed look, I'm guessing the drinks invite's off the board now. How do you do it, Nic? You're like honey to a bee.'

'My magnetic personality, babe. And it was a mutual decision to share the room, under the circumstances.'

'Of course it was,' she said, amused. 'You're obviously her hero. I'd hate you on behalf of all women if I didn't know you better.' She waved him off. 'Now go away. I'm too busy and too married to be sidetracked by a charmer like you.'

He grinned—charm had nothing to do with it. Fate had played right into his hands. Man, he had to love volcanoes. Even lousy reporters.

'And if you're not careful, Nic,' she was going on as she resumed her seat in front of her computer, 'one of these days you're going to find yourself charmed right back and life as you know it now will be a distant memory.'

He gave her a wave as he moved off. 'Not gonna happen.'

Kerry didn't look up from her screen. 'Uh-huh.'

He took the elevator, jogged across the sky bridge and onto grass, dodging passengers, following the arrivals road and outdoor car-parking, his mind reliving their up-close and the way Charlotte had responded. As if she couldn't get enough. He grinned to himself as he waited at the kerb for an airport bus, then crossed a median strip and headed for a line of bushes. Who'd have thought? Charlotte whoever-she-was was one hot babe.

And she was waiting in his room. *Their* room.

So what the hell was *he* waiting for? Why was he out running in this cold blustery wind when he could be getting better acquainted on that big wide bed with a woman who, if he was reading her right, wanted the same thing?

Because he'd already decided to run before she'd given him the hot look. Then chosen to take a damn shower—alone. She'd made it abundantly clear. She'd needed time. Fair enough. And now he thought about it, he wanted to give her that time to mull it over and be sure. Because *he* was sure he didn't want her backing out once they got started. In fact, he was so ready to get started, his body so tightly wound and hot, it was a wonder he could move at all.

In his experience conservative types in silk suits and pearls weren't compatible with one-night stands. But dress sense aside, she'd not played the distressed damsel card. The guy had been seriously hassling her but she'd held her own—like the strong heroines he portrayed in his computer games. He liked that about her. She wasn't afraid to stand up for herself even though he'd seen the flicker of panic in her eyes. So if she changed her mind, he reckoned she'd let him know.

Testosterone surged through him, tightening his muscles, pumping through his blood, and all he could think about was getting her naked and exploring the abundantly curved body he'd held against him. With his eyes, with his hands. With his mouth. Hell—he hoped she wasn't the type to change her mind.

He checked his watch. Time enough to have finished that shower. And if not…well, he'd just have to finish it with her. He turned back towards the hotel, making a detour via the terminal's food court on the way.

Since she'd already told the guy, and she'd needed the time to *breathe*, Charlotte took the shower. With no change of clothes available, and not wanting to crease her suit any more than it already was, she put the terry bathrobe provided by the hotel on over her underwear.

She swiped the mirror and stared at her reflection. Her mouth looked plumper, fuller. Her eyes looked bigger. More slumberous. *Bedroom eyes*. Oh, God. She rubbed a hand over her heart, which still hadn't settled into its usual rhythm. She'd never had a one-night stand before. Never been with another man before; Flynn had been a part of her life since her mid-teens.

Part of her life? *Huh.* She picked up her brush, dragged it through her hair with hard, swift strokes. Their relationship had been over less than two weeks when she'd seen him and the glamorous daughter of a wealthy businessman in the newspaper's social pages.

So she was getting on with her new life, starting today. She'd never met a guy's gaze—so full on and meaningful—the way she had Nic's just now. And he was coming back to *see how they got along.*

And with that look in his eyes it could mean only one thing: sex. Hot and fast and uncomplicated. Spontaneous. Frivolous. Happy. And wasn't that what she wanted too? Just for tonight. Then she'd never have to see him again.

Oh. My. Was that really Charlotte Dumont thinking those thoughts?

Swinging away from her unsettling image, she gathered her things and tentatively opened the door. Hearing no movement—so Nic hadn't returned yet—she walked into the bedroom.

Nic's backpack sat next to hers on the luggage rack; his spicy scent lingered on his discarded clothes on the back of the chair. He wasn't here yet he was all around her. She noticed some glossy brochures he'd left on the desk. She didn't want to get personally involved with him, wasn't ready for another relationship, but they were…just travel pamphlets. Nothing personal, nothing private. She couldn't resist picking them up.

The Hawaiian Islands. Brochures on deep-sea fishing, golf, whale-watching expeditions. The best surfing spots. He'd marked off some, made notes she couldn't decipher and crossed out others. He was on his way to Hawaii for what looked like a full-on guy vacation. No wonder he looked so fit. Bronzed. Well…nourished. He obviously knew how to chill out and have *fun*.

The word conjured up all sorts of scenarios; not the outdoor kind, but the intimate indoor kind involving him and her and that big bed with its soft white pillows. Her whole body burned. It wanted to burn alongside his. It wanted to know what it was like to be made love to by a man with Nic's expertise because one thing she was sure of was his ability to pleasure a woman. And then he'd be off to Hawaii and she'd be totally satisfied.

But it had to be her way. Her rules. No talking about themselves and their lives beyond what happened in this room. No swapping phone numbers and email addresses and promises to catch up. She didn't *want* him catching up. She wanted one night to prove to herself that she wasn't the girl Flynn thought she was.

Anticipation raced through her body. To calm herself, she made a cup of the complimentary coffee provided and slid the curtains back as the afternoon faded and the sky took on the early evening hues of orange and lavender. She sat on the only armchair and flicked through a women's magazine she'd bought earlier but she soon tossed it onto the nearby desk, too frazzled to concentrate on some superstar's private life exposed to the world.

And if it hadn't been for Nic, her private break-up with the popular candidate for the upcoming state elections might have been public fodder too.

She really, really owed Nic. So she could have just bought him a bottle of wine or a meal to show her appreciation, couldn't she? They were here until tomorrow morning at the earliest so it wasn't too late to suggest catching a cab into the city and finding some cosy candlelit café…

Except then they'd come back to this room and that bed

with a few glasses of happy in their systems and it would still be here—the amazing attraction.

She tucked her bare feet up beneath her, pulled the pins out of her hair and teased her fingers through it, enjoying the new feeling of being feminine and free. Why eat out when you could feast on something much more pleasurable right here? Like hot masculine skin and lips and tongues and… Her mouth dried, her skin frizzled. She couldn't help it; she giggled like a schoolgirl at the wicked thoughts running through her mind.

She was still giggling when he walked in.

CHAPTER THREE

NIC heard the feminine laughter as he pushed open the door. Husky with a hint of wicked. He grinned. Until he caught sight of her sitting on the chair, her face in profile as she stared out of the window, her dark hair aflame in the sun's reddening light and his amusement shifted beyond a simple *Wow* to something approaching awe. Unbound and auburn, the glossy mass rejoiced around her shoulders like a celebration of freedom.

She'd turned the TV on to a radio channel. Something soothing and blue and jazzy and she obviously hadn't heard him come in, so he absorbed the moment with all his senses. The fragrance of her recent shower, the delight in her laugh, her sheer and glorious abandonment.

And he realised he was witnessing something he doubted many people saw when they looked at Charlotte. The woman's inner beauty. And an innate sexuality that he found irresistible. He had a feeling she didn't show that side of herself often, much less share it.

He hoped she'd share it with him.

She'd swapped that seriously awful suit for the hotel's robe. Was she naked underneath? His groin tightened. She still wore the pearls; their iridescence reflected the sun's vermilion rays. He imagined lifting them, warm from her body, and sliding his fingers beneath to explore her creamy throat.

He couldn't be certain she'd changed into the robe as an invitation or prelude to sex. It made sense that she'd wear it since their luggage was checked in at the airport. But that was about the only thing that made sense right now because for the life of him he couldn't remember ever being this captivated by a woman before.

Again the sense that this was different—*she* was different—slid through him like a ripple on a millpond. He shook off the shivery silvery sensation and discreetly cleared his throat to announce his presence. 'Anyone for soggy gourmet pizza?'

She swung to face him and a thousand different emotions flitted over her expression before she settled for happy-to-see-him. 'Yes, please.' She uncurled herself and stretched out a pair of long shapely legs in front of her. 'Where did you find pizza?'

'The airport's café. The last one. Or the last half of one. I had to fight off the hungry hordes.' After setting the box on the desk, he switched on the lamp, then reached for the bottle of wine on the shelf above the bar fridge.

She rose, smiling and shrugging the lapels of the robe closer. 'My hero.'

His hand jerked a bit at that as he upended two glasses. 'You want wine?'

'Thanks.' She lifted the lid on the cardboard container. 'Yum, I love artichokes.' She peered closer. 'It *is* artichoke, isn't it?'

He grinned. 'I think so.'

She reached for her handbag on the coffee table, pulled out a linen napkin embroidered with her name, then proceeded to polish up the motel's cutlery.

Swallowing his surprise, he opened the bottle, then set

a couple of paper plates next to the pizza box. 'You like Italian?'

'I do, but seafood's my favourite.' She scooped up the slices with a knife, set them on the plates. 'There's a fabulous seafood place at Glenelg, on the Marina Pier. Their King George whiting is to die for.'

'I know the one.' He didn't tell her his apartment overlooked said pier as he splashed a generous amount of the ruby liquid into the glasses. 'And I agree with your review. It's one of my favourite food haunts when I'm in Adelaide.'

'Mine too.' A little hitch in her breath as she stared up at him. 'Seems we have something in common.'

'I'm hoping that's not all we have in common.' He couldn't resist stroking his knuckles lightly down the side of her face. Testing her, tormenting himself. Her skin was smooth as silk and smelled like flowers.

Her eyes turned glassy, like a still ocean on an overcast summer's day, and she pressed her lips together, then said, 'We weren't going to talk about ourselves.'

'Who said anything about talking?'

Their gazes clashed, but he didn't act on the hot fist of anticipation gripping the lower half of his body and the impulse to show her the alternative option. Plenty of time. A girl like Charlotte definitely needed slow. And he'd already made up his mind to give her a chance to decide whether she still wanted to act on that hot look he'd glimpsed earlier.

So he only lifted the glasses, offered her one and said, 'Let's eat before this sloppy offering gets any colder. Cheers.'

'Thanks. And cheers.' Taking her plate, Charlotte returned to the armchair while Nic sat at the desk. She took a sip, then set her glass on the coffee table in front of her. Her cheek was still tingly and warm from his touch. Other parts were tingling too, with a wickedly wanton need like she'd never experienced.

But he was giving her space and she appreciated that. Even if she was having a full-on fantasy around him and what they could get up to on that office chair...

'Hawaii's nice this time of year,' she said to take her mind off her fantasies, determined to keep the conversation on neutral topics.

He glanced at his pamphlets then at her, his gaze thoughtful. Unreadable.

'I know we agreed on nothing personal but they were just there...'

He smiled, all trace of whatever she'd seen in his eyes gone in one mischievous twinkle. 'All good, Charlotte, it's not personal. And yeah, it's the best time of year. Get away from the cold.' He bit off half his slice in one go and chewed, then washed it down with a mouthful of wine.

She sliced a corner off her own piece, watching the man's enthusiasm over the very ordinary food. He had a strong tanned neck and prominent Adam's apple, which moved as he swallowed. Oil from the pizza glistened on his upper lip... She wanted to jump up, lean down and lick it off. She really needed to slow her thoughts down to warp speed.

'You've been there before?' she asked, keeping to the script.

'I try to make it every couple of years. Hanalei Bay on Kauai. The surf's great there. How about you—have you ever been?'

'Once. To Maui. It was a family holiday to celebr...' She trailed off as the memory of her parents' tenth wedding anniversary surfaced. The little twinge in her heart had her rubbing her hand once over the area and caressing the pearls at her throat. 'But that's against the rules.'

'Sure—if you say so.' His eyes probed hers and his voice gentled. 'You okay?'

'Fine.' Her smile relaxed as she finished the last bite, patted her mouth then popped the fancy napkin back in her bag. 'You know, you're a very nice man.'

'Nice?' His brows rose. 'That's a bit of a worry.'

'I mean honest. Considerate…' Totally gorgeous.

He chuckled and popped the remainder of his pizza into his mouth. 'You sure you're not a rebellious princess on the run from some minor European nation somewhere?'

'What? Oh, the napkin?' She grinned back. 'I'd carry my own cutlery if the airlines allowed it. I have personalised soap too. Somewhere…' She searched the bottom of her bag unsuccessfully, then shrugged. 'Call me eccentric.' Or a product of a privileged and traditional upbringing. If her folks could see her now and knew what she was thinking…

She bet Nic had a string of women in his life. She wondered how old he was. Around thirty? She reminded herself she didn't want to know because then she'd want to know more. Like where he lived and what his work was and…how he liked to make love.

'"Sex Fact or Fiction".'

She almost spluttered into her wine. 'Pardon?'

'The quiz.' He was looking at the cover of the magazine she'd left on the desk. 'You haven't read it yet?'

'I must've missed it. Obviously you didn't.'

'I'm a guy. I saw the word sex,' he said, amusement in his voice as he flicked through the pages. 'Okay, test your knowledge. Sales of condoms decrease when a recession hits—fact or fiction?'

She took a moment to compose herself and consider. 'Fiction. Definitely. Too expensive to go out and too expensive to have kids.'

He nodded. 'Correct. How about this? Humans are the only species to have sex for pleasure.'

The way he said 'pleasure', all virile and velvet and promising, made her skin rupture with heat. She took another sip of wine. 'Yes.'

'Not so.' He studied her with inscrutable eyes. 'Apparently we're not the only creatures on the planet wanting to get it on.'

'Oh?' But was she the only one in this room right now wanting to get it on? He was as relaxed as if he was discussing the weather, one arm slung over the back of the chair, whereas she was as tense as strung piano wire.

'How about this, then? Men's sexual organs are designed for more pleasure than women's.'

'Um…' She trailed off at the hot promise of that pleasure. Her own feminine places dampened and she had to resist squirming on the chair. 'Fiction.'

'Yep. Women have it all over men in this department. According to the quiz, the clitoris is the only known organ that exists for the sole purpose of pleasure.'

Oh. Her cheeks felt as if they were on fire. Had she ever had such a bizarrely intimate conversation with a guy before? 'Um…sexual organs aside…' she bit down on her bottom lip '…surely it would depend on who's giving the pleasure?'

His head came up and he looked at her through lazy-lidded eyes. 'You're a woman—you tell me.'

'For me…' She struggled for composure and sophistication. 'It definitely depends on the partner.'

'Wouldn't this partner's expertise have something to do with it? Besides liking the guy.'

'Ah…'

'I mean, you could be totally hot for him but if he doesn't know how to do it for you… Ever had a guy like that? You really like him, the connection's there, the spark, the desire, but then you're left hanging. So to speak.'

'Uh…hmm.' *Flynn*. The earth hadn't exactly moved with him. Ever. She'd told herself that was okay because she'd loved him, and love and affection and common goals were more important than physical fulfilment.

Maybe she'd been wrong, because there'd been a shifting of tectonic plates happening beneath her feet since she'd kissed Nic. She knew instinctively that he wouldn't be the type to leave any woman unsatisfied.

'What's this non-committal "hmm"?'

'It's a yes, okay?' she snapped out, hating to admit it. Hating that he knew already. 'I've had guys like that.'

A slow and sexy, won't-happen-if-you're-with-me look drifted across his expression.

If he ever decided to make a move.

And why was this all about her? His focus was entirely too…focused. She deflected with, 'But a guy can enjoy sex with anyone because it's all about basic drive or need, right?'

His gaze drifted over her like slow-moving lava. 'Personally speaking, I like to connect with the woman I'm with. Enjoyment has to be about more than satisfying a basic urge. I feel a connection with you, Charlotte. I'm pretty sure you feel that connection too. I'd like to see where it takes us.'

To heaven and beyond?

His eyes had darkened as he spoke and she felt a shifting and thickening of anticipation in the air. But he didn't move. Not so much as the flicker of an eyelash.

Ah. 'Are you waiting for me to give you the green light?'

'Your call.' He remained ostensibly at ease, legs sprawled in front of him, arm still relaxed on the back of the chair. Only a muscle tic in his jaw betrayed his tension. 'You need to be sure this is what you want. But for pity's sake, make it soon.' His voice thickened and he looked down at his crotch. 'Because you're damn near killing me.'

She'd deliberately kept her eyes above his waist, but now she followed his gaze to the impressive bulge in his shorts. And swallowed. Her whole body went weak, except for her galloping pulse. She also noticed his thighs were as tanned as his neck, sprinkled with dark hair and heavy with muscle as if he worked out. A lot.

She wanted to touch. She wanted to feel those thighs rub against hers. She wanted that magnificent masculine part of him inside her.

But she didn't want entanglements. No morning after, no getting to know each other beyond the physical. 'Only tonight.'

'Fine. Should I take a shower first?'

'No.' She smiled. 'Told you you're considerate.' She liked the way he smelled: warm and slightly sweaty but not unpleasant. A primal masculine smell that beckoned and aroused her feminine instincts. 'I want it—I want you—as you are. I want to feel your sweat on my skin. Now.'

He smiled back. 'First move's all yours.'

'Mine?' Her trembling fingers tightened a little on the soft terry lapels. She knew how to initiate sex...but with a man like Nic? Except she didn't know Nic, not really. So what did she mean: 'a man like Nic'? What did Nic-who-she-didn't-know want or expect?

'You could start by taking off that robe,' he suggested after a few seconds of silence ticked by. 'Or you could come over here and let me do the honours.' Still he didn't move. 'I'll leave that decision to you.'

Eyes fastened on him, she pushed up off the chair. The few steps she took seemed like miles while her blood drained to her legs. She was glad of the background music because it covered the sound of her heart thumping its way out of her chest. Not with fear but with the illicit, dizzying prospect of having sex with a man who was, by anyone's standards, a stranger.

She was the one in control—because Nic had given it to her. She was the one with the choice. And she wanted this night with this man.

Coming to a stop in front of him, she loosened the looped tie just enough so that the robe's front edges parted slightly. As she was standing, his head was tilted back a little, eyes focused on hers, and it was her first chance to look down at him. She reached out and smoothed a strand of his hair off his brow. 'Decisions, decisions…'

He slid his fingers behind the loop in her belt and drew her closer, between hot, hard thighs, and she had to drop her hands onto the chair's metal arms either side of him to keep her balance and stop herself from collapsing onto him.

His breath, his scent and his heat mingled with hers as they continued to stare at each other. 'You like being on top, then.'

She started to laugh but her throat was dry and it came out husky and low and slightly desperate. 'I like being any way.'

Oh, my God. Had she really said that? And was that smoky, seductive voice hers?

'So…' he untied her belt and slipped his hands inside to lightly circle her waist, surprise in his eyes when he found bare flesh '…swinging naked from the chandelier's a possibility?'

Her breath hitched at the feather-light brush of skin on skin and she arched forward, her breasts aching to be teased and stroked. 'No chandelier here…' Only recessed lighting and a desk lamp…

'Pity.'

'But whatever we get up to, do you have protection?' Her mind was hazy, but not that hazy.

'We'll get to that. Eventually. Or are you in a rush?'

'I thought *you* were. Didn't you just say—?'

'I'll survive a little longer.'

She wondered if she would. Spot-fires were breaking out all over her body; it was a miracle she wasn't glowing. Or perhaps she was but right now she was too distracted watching Nic. His expression: part pain, part pleasure and all for her. 'Nic...'

'Charlotte...' he teased back and his tone left her in no doubt he was as turned on as she. But he withdrew his hands from her waist, put them behind his head. 'What are you hiding under all that towelling?'

She pushed up off the chair's support and straightened, then, with a boldness she'd never felt, she shrugged off the robe. Its coarse texture tickled her bare skin on the way down.

Nic watched, his breath snagging on a growl of approval. Who'd have thought? Conservative Charlotte liked sexy underwear. Skimpy shimmery panties and bra, spattered with starbursts of silver rhinestones and so sheer she might as well have been naked. But so much more erotic with her dark, peaked nipples pushed up against the fabric, her breasts spilling over the top like an offering of abundance. The strand of pearls still luminescent at her neck.

'Aren't you full of surprises,' he murmured in absolute appreciation. 'Gorgeous.'

But not too voluptuous. Not too slim either; just long, strong, clean lines and curves. Perfect. Exquisite. It was a crime against mankind to hide such beauty.

But she wasn't hiding it from him.

She resumed her earlier position, hands on the armrests, leaning over him. Her breasts were at eye-level and with any other woman that was where he'd be—mouth busy right there on that creamy skin, teasing the fabric aside with his teeth, tongue exploring.

But, as delectable as they were, it was her eyes that captured him most. Wide and aware with smoke and secrets shifting like shadows. Her fragrance, the cool, light signature perfume, drifted over him like evening mist. And in his mind's eye he saw that calm lake at sunset. If he believed in enchantment, he imagined it would be like this.

Behind his head, his fists tightened. He put them on his thighs to stop himself from reaching up and pulling her mouth down to his and plundering. He sensed her willingness but this wasn't the moment for fast. Rather a moment for reflection.

She hadn't admitted it, but Nic knew this wasn't something Charlotte did casually and often. He didn't linger on the reasons why she'd made an exception for him. 'You're not used to this, are you?' he murmured, and heard her quick exhalation, felt the tension thrum through her body.

'What do you mean? Sex?'

'One-night sex.'

'Is it that obvious?'

'No, no.' He kept his voice low and slow and soothing. 'I mean that in a good way. Keep doing what you're doing—you're fantastic.'

He shook away the unsettling thoughts and concentrated on what he knew well. How to enjoy no-strings, uncomplicated sex. And the easy pleasure of having a woman initiate it.

Smiling, she lowered her lips to his, a slow sultry kiss that soothed and smoothed and seduced. Her hair was a curtain of silk around them and the bluesy pulse of the music beat a lazy syrupy rhythm. He thought of languid afternoons by a pool and hot skin and cold, creamy sunscreen.

He lifted his arms then, fingers spread to mould around her slender shoulders and draw her closer. Her fingers stroked through his hair, then cupped the back of his head. Still watching his eyes. There was a glide of silk as she parted her long, long legs and slid them over his thighs to twine herself around him. She hooked her feet behind the back of the chair, the sultry heat of her feminine core snug against his burning erection.

Still holding his head, she leaned forward and kissed him again, her sparkly bra snagging his T-shirt as she settled closer. A groan erupted from deep in his gut. Her smile was smug as she found the worn jersey's hem and tugged upwards. Suddenly his T-shirt was gone, flung somewhere over his shoulder.

Her fingers danced over his chest, twirled around his nipples, then slowed to a gliding waltz and headed south, dead centre. To the waistband of his shorts. Hands diving beneath, she rocked once against him, her fingers tightening on their captured prize. 'Nic...'

'Okay, now you're playing dirty.' He reached behind her, snapped the catch on her bra and peeled it away. Creamy flesh, dark, ripe peaks. Greed hazed his vision but she didn't give him time to feast, surging forward to rub the hard little nubs against his chest as she watched him.

'I like playing dirty, don't you?' Her laugh was low and sexy as she massaged and squeezed. 'Fast and dirty even better.'

He tried to laugh too, but it snagged in his throat. His control was fraying, his whole body one throbbing ache. 'You're a wicked woman.'

'Too wicked for you?'

'Not possible.' He cupped her damp heat and watched

her eyes smoulder, her playful smile fade to serious. Her hands stopped being busy and he grinned. 'Pay-back time.' He slid a finger along the edge of her panties and felt her shudder. He slipped beneath to stroke her slick flesh and heard her moan. Arousal heightened, breathing quickened.

Somehow he managed to reach over his shoulder and drag his trousers off the chair, fumbling for his wallet and a condom in the rumpled folds while he thanked the stars his clothes were within reach.

Impatience, desperation and demands and needs. He freed himself, rolled on protection. A quick tug and her panties shredded beneath his fingers. No laughter now, no teasing wordplay. Just pure passion and dark desire and every fantasy he'd ever had. He plunged deep, thrusting up into silky heat and willing delight.

He held her silvery gaze long enough to see that her response matched his own. He gripped her hips, her hands fisted in his hair. They found their rhythm. The world evaporated leaving only speed and greed and heat.

The chair rocked beneath them. He thought he heard the tinkle of a glass as it toppled and rolled but maybe it was the sound of his sanity shattering.

She came on a stunned gasp, her inner muscles clamping around him. He gave himself up to glory and followed.

CHAPTER FOUR

SHE hadn't been able to get enough of him, Nic thought hours later as night moved inexorably towards dawn. Nor he her. And why not? Making the most of the time limit she'd imposed. He turned his head to watch her sleep. Hair in disarray around her face, over the pillow. The gentle sound of her breathing as her breasts rose and fell. Her cool blue fragrance was going to tease his nostrils and his memory for quite some time.

He felt entirely too relaxed to worry about the curious little niggle that it had never been quite like this with anyone before. That *connection* he'd so casually mentioned to entice her? It had been...well...more than he'd expected.

He shifted onto an elbow for a better look at her bathed in the gold of dawn. His fingers itched to stroke the side of her face, her lips, her hair. He wanted her again. Wanted to feel her tight, hot wetness clench around him as she came... Wanted to look into those haunting eyes she had and— He frowned. Maybe he wasn't as relaxed as he'd thought. But it would pass, he assured himself. Of course it would. And she'd made it clear enough: one night. He'd been happy with the arrangement. More than happy.

Okay, he decided on a slow breath of relief, sanity still intact after all. They'd shared a fantastic few hours but it was time to make a move towards getting out of here.

Careful not to disturb her, he rose and went to the bathroom, checked his mobile for updates to flight schedules, then showered and left her sleeping while he went in search of breakfast.

Charlotte woke to the hum of air conditioning and the sound of water running in the bathroom. She didn't move for a long moment, reliving the night and all she and Nic had done together. She'd lost count of how many times he'd made her come.

But his side of the bed was empty now, the sheets barely warm to the touch. She felt a vague disappointment that he'd not woken her earlier, then stretched. Aah… She'd expended more energy than she'd realised, she thought as her eyes slid open on a clear dawn sky, steadily lightening with gold and aqua. She should include sex in her exercise regime.

'Rise and shine.' Nic appeared freshly shaved and dressed. 'The ash cloud's shifted. Flights resume in an hour or so. We need to get moving.'

'What time is it?' she murmured, *without* moving. She was way too naked beneath the sheet, and her underwear—she had no idea where it was.

'Six-thirty.'

She groaned into the pillow.

He had a way too cheery wide-awake voice. Obviously he was raring to get to Hawaii and begin his surfing vacation, that basic sexual drive they'd talked about last night satisfied for now.

And he'd satisfied her too but it was finished.

In one way she mourned the fact, in another, she was so, so relieved. Because last night Charlotte Dumont's body had been invaded by a nymphomaniac. In fact, now she was almost too embarrassed to look him in the eye, and a warm blush suffused her entire body.

She tried her best to ignore it. 'Is that coffee I smell? *Real* coffee?'

'Cappuccino or latte?' Still managing to look crisp in yesterday's clothes, he lifted a couple of paper cups with lids from the desk. 'I didn't know what you liked so I bought one of each.'

'I'd love the latte, please. You've been out already?'

'Organisation, babe.' He moved to the bed, held out a cup and a small plastic shopping bag from one of the terminal's tourist shops. 'You might need these too.'

Propping herself up on one elbow, she peeked inside. She glimpsed a pair of lolly-pink panties with a map of Australia imprinted on the front. Oh, dear. And the reason she was going to be wearing tacky nylon souvenir undies for the rest of the day spun through her mind like hot-pink candy floss. 'Um. Thanks.'

'It's for my own peace of mind as much as yours. I'd go nuts with the mental image of you buck naked under that skirt all day and not being able to take advantage.'

The candy-floss colour bled into her cheeks. She sat up, winding the sheet up around her torso as she did so. 'Oh…well, then…'

Head on one side, he studied her a moment. 'There's something intriguing about a woman reclining naked in bed wearing only pearls. You've got me wondering: why pearls?'

'They were my mother's. And I'm not reclining. Now.' Sentimental secrets were not up for sharing. Setting the cup on the night stand, she scrunched the sheet higher. 'Um…'

He must have known what she couldn't ask because he picked her bra up from the bottom of the bed and tossed it to her. The glint in his eyes dissipated as he studied her. 'Everything okay?'

'Yes. Fine. Why wouldn't it be?'

'You look—'

'I'm going to take a shower,' she said, all casual and carefree. But she didn't move. Her fingers couldn't seem to let go of the sheet. She'd not given a thought to the morning after the night before. Whatever would he be thinking of her?

And why did it matter? In less than an hour they'd say goodbye and that would be it. She just had to get through this awkward time, then she could relax and enjoy her holiday.

'Better make it snappy.' Checking his watch, he rose, picked up his bag and headed towards the door. 'See you in the lobby in fifteen minutes.'

She was grateful for his sensitivity to her unspoken need for privacy despite the fact that he'd seen, touched and tasted nearly every naked inch of her, but the blush still hadn't cooled when she found him downstairs amongst the swirl of people. Her hand dived into her bag for her sunglasses.

He swung his pack onto one shoulder, setting a cracking pace across the sky bridge with a trail of other passengers and leaving no breath for small talk.

They arrived inside the terminal. 'Thanks for everything,' she said, well before they reached her check-in desk. 'Um…I meant rescuing me and all…' She trailed off. All, indeed.

'My pleasure.' His dark eyes twinkled in the harsh down-lights.

Mine too. She rolled her lips together before she said too much. 'So…I…guess it's…goodbye, then.'

'Let's just say *au revoir*, babe.'

He bent to brush a chaste kiss across her lips. There was something about his expression when he straightened that sent a little shiver down her spine, but then before she could look into his dark velvet eyes one more time he turned and walked away, disappearing into the crowd.

Biting down on her lower lip, she fought an urgent impulse to call him back. Memories of his heat-slicked body against hers, their fevered moans and air ripe with passion swarmed through her mind. But more than that, he'd come to her assistance when she'd needed it, no questions asked. Why was she letting this man walk out of her life with almost no possibility of finding him again?

She started after him, but a couple of steps on she realised it was too late. The terminal was teeming with chaos and commotion; she'd never find him and she ran the risk of missing her flight. And even if she caught up with him, what could she say? What *was* there to say?

They'd shared one fantastic night. But the probability of him wanting more wasn't a probability at all or he'd have tried harder to get her contact details. If he'd wanted to, he'd have persisted, found a way— men were like that. But he'd not asked her once. Not once. Happy to walk away. She told herself she was *not* disappointed.

Charlotte was grateful for the comfort and relative privacy of the spacious Tabua Class window seat at the front of the aircraft. She didn't have to look at other passengers, and the seat next to her was vacant. She plugged in her music player, closed her eyes and drifted...

Cold... Charlotte rubbed her arms against the aircraft's air conditioning, fighting sleep and the images that had plagued her for the past six weeks.

Flynn in her kitchen, impossibly handsome, and telling her, 'I've decided to stand as a candidate for the next state election.'

'You what...? Politics?' She struggled to process his announcement. 'I thought you were just networking at the electorate, volunteering your skills. That it was part of your business plan for our wine and cheese place...'

'There's not going to be a place, Charlotte.'

A chill swept down her spine. 'But your viticulture course...'

'I switched courses last year.'

'And you didn't tell me?' Everything was spiralling away. 'You didn't bother to tell *your fiancée you were considering a career in politics*?' Who was this man she'd thought she knew? 'What happened to sharing? How could you shut me out that way?'

'I know how you feel about being in the public eye.' He shrugged. 'And frankly, being married to a little grey mouse isn't going to work for a future politician.'

And she felt herself shrivel beneath his critical scrutiny. The guy who'd seduced her at sixteen with his flashing green eyes, his smooth words and good looks stared at her now with chauvinistic intolerance.

'Take a look at yourself, Charlotte.' His gaze crawled up her body once more. 'Take a good look at this place.' He waved a disparaging hand around her kitchen. 'You're living in a damn time warp. I need a wife who'll stand by me into the future. A woman who knows how to make a fashion statement. One with some backbone who's not afraid to speak up in public.'

The utter betrayal of everything she'd ever believed in about him. About *them*.

She jolted awake as the aircraft hit turbulence. Or maybe it was her stomach still tying itself in knots over his harsh words. So she concentrated on watching the twisting ribbon of surf along the coast as the aircraft began its descent into Nadi. Flynn had used her position in society to build connections, then tossed her aside.

Little grey mouse.

She ground her teeth together as a patchwork of different greens came into view. Last night she'd proved she was confident and capable of being whoever she wanted to be. She should thank Flynn for the wake-up call.

She watched the brown river snake below them—palm trees rippling in the afternoon breeze, hazy smoke spirals towards the bony ridges of distant highlands—and drew in a deep breath. New horizons and some time to blow away the cobwebs.

She stepped out into the moist tropical air and followed her fellow passengers across the hot tarmac and into the terminal. Four locals in bright shirts with hibiscus flowers behind their ears welcomed them with white smiles and their pretty yellow banjos, dreamy island harmonies blending.

'*Bula!*' Welcome.

'*Vinaka.*' Thank you.

Smiling at the pretty ground staff member in her *Sulu Jaba*, the traditional long skirt topped with a bright fitted dress, Charlotte headed for the baggage carousel and collected her luggage. She loved Fiji already. A place where she knew no one and no one knew her...

That thought vanished with a sharp inhalation when she caught sight of a pair of broad shoulders encased in a familiar dark shirt near the carousel. Her heart jumped into her mouth and every muscle seemed to melt. She watched him pull his bag off the conveyor, bronzed forearms, muscles twisting.

Nic.

She couldn't move, and against her will her eyes drank in the sight. His tall, tanned, testosterone-packed body, the long lanky stride as he walked towards Customs. What was he doing in Fiji? A connecting flight? Except he'd collected his luggage already.

Conflicting emotions tore through her like a summer cyclone. The swoon effect of remembering that body naked and stretched over hers and the chill factor of realising he'd deliberately misled her about Hawaii. Heat flared like a furnace, burning her cheeks.

She didn't *want* to see him again. But her body had other ideas and called her a liar. Her breasts tingled with remembered pleasure, her inner thighs quivered with the memory of the warm dampness of his mouth there.

No. Yes. No. She really tried to look away but it was as if her eyes were pre-programmed to follow him. The one-off fantasy man she'd allowed herself to indulge in.

Hadn't he indulged in her too? Seemed, like her ex, he was also one of those smooth-talking rogues who knew how to seduce a woman and make it seem as if it was all *her* idea. She didn't know how he'd managed it but he had.

She proceeded through Customs keeping well behind him but damned if he wasn't standing smack bang in front of the exit doors talking on his mobile when she emerged. How was she going to get past him? Or was that his intention?

Then, as if sensing her watching—condemning—he looked over his shoulder and met her eyes, and she wished she'd turned away already because now it was too late, she was powerless against the pull.

Not taking his eyes off her, he spoke to whoever he was talking with on the phone and disconnected. He started walking towards her.

Was he *smiling* when he knew she didn't want anything more to do with him? They'd had an arrangement, they'd said goodbye... No—she'd said goodbye, she remembered. He'd made a point of saying *au revoir*. She didn't know how he'd found out her intended destination, but he'd *known* and he'd said nothing.

Her head spun. Was he a reporter too and she'd just been totally made a fool of…?

She was ready when he reached her. She was strong. She was cool. 'What are you doing here?'

He slung his backpack to the floor, all charm and smiles. 'What one usually does here in Fiji—relax and enjoy.'

'You lied to me.'

His brow furrowed, those eyes all innocence. 'Lied?'

'You said you were going to Hawaii.'

'No. You *assumed* I was going to Hawaii.'

She tried to recall the conversation but right now her mind wasn't operating at full capacity because it was too busy looking at the way his gorgeous lips curved ever so slightly. Teasing her. Or was he mocking her? 'And you let me,' she clipped out. 'We talked about it, you let me believe—'

'You asked if I'd been there before. I said I try to get there every couple of years. Just not this year, as it happens.'

'You knew exactly what I meant.' She frowned. 'You didn't tell me you were travelling to Fiji when we talked about Hawaii.'

'Why would I? No exchanging personal information. Your rules, Charlotte, remember?' he said softly. Seductively. The way he'd whispered how good she felt and what else he'd like to do to her.

'I didn't see you in the airline lounge in Melbourne or in Customs…'

'That was my intention. You were adamant you only wanted one night, no further services required.'

She felt herself colour at his crude assessment of the evening. Obviously it would seem that way to him and why should he believe her if she tried to explain? But rather than special, he made their night together sound cheap and sordid and ruined the memory and she resented him for that.

'I'd have been better off facing up to that reporter,' she said tightly.

He gave her a grin that twisted her insides into a tight little ball again. 'Charlotte, come on. Loosen up a bit.'

She could read it in his eyes—*the way you were twelve hours ago*. Her chin lifted. 'What about now? You're not trying to avoid me *now*. In fact you're making it your business to catch up with me.' Her eyes narrowed. 'Maybe you're a reporter too and you were in on this together.'

'You don't really think that.' He blew out a breath, looked about them. 'Why don't we find somewhere more private to talk—?'

'No more private.' She would not give in to the temptation and tightened her fingers on the handle of her suitcase. 'Right here's fine.'

'Okay.' He raised a hand as if to touch her face, then changed his mind, lowered it again. 'I've been thinking about you for the entire flight. And I wondered if maybe you've changed your mind. Because I'd really like to see you again while we're both here.'

'I didn't come to Fiji to meet someone. I came here to be alone.'

'A shameful waste of romantic sunsets, don't you think?'

'No.' She could enjoy sunsets; she didn't need a man for that. And she refused to think what she did need a man for... So she didn't think about how hard and hairy his forearm would feel if she reached out and touched it. She ignored his familiar masculine scent, arousing now in the humid air wafting through the exit doors. And she totally didn't think about the dark, drugging taste of his kisses, the way his eyes had glittered down at her in the dark, jaw clenched as he came inside her.

'Admit it, Charlotte, you enjoyed our time together as much as I did.' His voice was deep velvet and pure seduction. 'It could be even better on a balmy tropical night with the windows open, the breeze wafting over hot damp skin...'

'Yes,' she snapped, not allowing herself to be tempted by the images he conjured. 'Not the bit about *better*—' she waved a jerky hand in front of her '—I meant last night. I admit it, okay? But that was last night.'

'And you're thinking how much you'd like to do it again.'

'You...you're way too sure of yourself.'

'You prefer a less confident man?'

'I prefer to be *alone* as I already told you. Men are not on my agenda right now.'

'Yet you made an exception for me.' He grinned. 'I'm flattered.'

'Don't be.' She pushed the words out. 'You were available, you were convenient and I used you. I used you *shamelessly*. A one-off. Nothing more.' She forced herself to look into his eyes and not crumple into a mindless mess. She even managed a smile—not too difficult when escape was just beyond those doors. 'I hope you enjoy your vacation. Goodbye.'

'I've got a car waiting. At least let me give you a lift to your hotel. Where are you staying?'

'I've organised for a car from the resort to collect me. In fact, he'll be wondering where I am.' She started walking, made a show of looking at her watch while noticing most of the passengers from their flight had already left the terminal.

'I'll walk you out.'

Trailing her suitcase, she headed for the exit, not looking at Nic walking beside her. While she scanned the area
for her ride, she saw Nic signal a shiny limo, which immediately drove to the kerb. The chauffeur who stepped
out was middle-aged and wore smart traditional clothing.

He grinned, teeth white against his dusky skin. 'Hey,
Nic. *Bula vinaka!*'

'Malakai, *bula.*'

Charlotte watched on, surprise mingling with confusion
as the pair clasped hands and greeted each other as if they
were old friends. 'Another resort guest on your flight is
riding with us,' she heard the chauffeur say, looking about.
'I don't see her yet.'

Nic looked her way and said slowly, 'Vaka Malua Resort
by any chance?'

Oh, no. She couldn't believe it. Then she noticed the
colours of the hotel's logo in the man's attire—turquoise,
black and ivory. Of all the resorts she could have chosen...
She nodded once. Fate was truly punishing her.

Nic said something to the other man in a low voice, then
stepped up and took her bags, swung them into the limo's
boot and said, 'Charlotte, this is Malakai.'

Malakai flashed his wide smile for her and opened the
car door. '*Bula*, ma'am. Welcome to Fiji.'

'Hello. *Bula.*' She forced a smile for him but her mind
was scrambled as she walked towards the vehicle.

Maybe she'd make some sense of it when she could finally close the door to her suite and block out the rest of the
world. Vaka Malua was a new luxury resort and, according to its website, spacious and private. She had her own
personal plunge pool and a view overlooking the sea. If she
chose, she could avoid the other tourists. Nic, for instance.

Nic waited until she'd climbed into the vehicle, then
made a snap decision and slid in beside Charlotte, en-

suring plenty of space between them. She was giving off vibes that would have most fellow passengers diving for the seat next to the driver, and under normal circumstances he would have enjoyed catching up with Malakai. But he knew it was all a front designed to keep him at a distance when what she really wanted was for him to touch her again.

As they headed south from Nadi towards the Coral Coast and Natadola Beach he carried on a running conversation with Malakai, but his mind was on the passenger sitting stiffly beside him.

He didn't believe Charlotte's talk about a convenient fling for a second. He knew women and she wasn't the type. He'd manipulated the situation to his advantage. So she was understandably annoyed with him, but even behind her invisible shield he could feel the pull between them.

Unlike him, she obviously came from old money. A rich babe with something to hide? He'd seen the emotion cloud her pretty grey eyes when she'd talked about her mother's pearls and the family holiday in Hawaii. Family was obviously important to her.

She claimed she didn't want anything to do with him. He had forty minutes or so to work on that. He pressed the button and the limo's window slid partway down, letting in the welcome fragrance of the tropics. 'Have you been to Fiji before, Charlotte?'

'No.'

He laid an arm across the back of the seat and angled himself so he could see her better. 'First impressions?'

'Friendly. Relaxing…I hope.' She sniffed the inrushing air. 'What's burning?'

'Sugar cane. They burn off before harvesting.' Her hair was tied back but strands were escaping and twirling around her temples. He only had to lift a finger and he'd be able to touch it but she was just starting to relax. 'Is the breeze bothering you?'

She shook her head. 'You know the driver,' she murmured.

'I'm a regular visitor to Fiji and Vaka Malua. Malakai's worked there since the resort opened.'

'Okay…so what does *Vaka Malua* mean?'

He looked into her eyes and said, 'It means to linger, or stay awhile.'

Of course it did—he could read the scepticism in her eyes. She held his gaze a split second longer, then turned away to let the air blow on her face.

He smiled to himself and turned to watch the Fijian green slide by before looking back at her. 'Do you travel a lot?'

'Not for the past couple of years.'

'How long are you here?' *How long do I have to convince you to change your mind?*

'Two weeks.'

'Well, I hope you find what you're looking for.'

She didn't reply.

Sensing she wasn't going to open up, he used the rest of the journey to provide a running commentary of the area they were passing through. Large cream dwellings set back from the road amongst encroaching vegetation, purple and red flamed bushes and stands of banana palms. The regular abundance of locals walked along the side of the road.

The resort came into view, a cluster of steep-pitched grey roofs in the traditional way of Fijian architecture, the Vaka Malua Club's deluxe bures perched on the top of the hill, the rest of the resort sweeping down to the beach.

Malakai pulled under the portico and the wide open-air reception area. 'You getting out here too?' he asked Nic.

'No.' He turned to Charlotte as Malakai slid out to open her door. 'Here we are. I have something to take care of elsewhere.' He nodded towards the staff approaching with smiles and banjos and shell necklaces. 'Looks like the welcome party's ready to cater to your every wish and command.'

She looked quickly at him and her eyes flashed hot—as he'd intended them to with his mention of wishes—before her gaze darted away to her handbag, which she'd strategically placed on the seat between them. 'I hope you enjoy your visit,' she said, climbing out.

'You too.' He watched her departure, unable to stop his gaze from wandering. She had the sexiest backside he'd ever come into contact with.

She was going to be here two weeks.

'Wait.' Flipping open his wallet, he pulled out an Aussie fifty-dollar note and scrawled his phone number across the bottom. He jumped out, came around to her side of the limo and tucked it in the top of her handbag. 'In case you change your mind.'

Without waiting for her response, he climbed back into the limo and shut the door. 'Take me home, Malakai.'

Smiling, he wondered who'd give in first.

CHAPTER FIVE

'THE new furniture arrived safely?' Nic talked freely now they were alone and heading for Nic's residence adjacent to the resort along a private road crowded with lush vegetation.

'Ni mataka,' Malakai told him. Tomorrow. 'It was sent to the resort by error this afternoon. They promised to come back in the morning.'

'And the artwork's finished?'

'Io.' Yes. 'Tenika likes the paintings very much.' Malakai spoke with shy fondness of his wife. 'We hung it like you said. Very nice.'

'I'm looking forward to seeing it.'

Nic was also looking forward to catching up with the couple who occupied a separate wing of his home, keeping the whole place spotless and liveable whenever he was down south, which was often weeks at a time. It was so satisfying to be in a position to provide two people he cared about with employment and accommodation. He knew how it was to live in poverty.

Moments later they drove through the high gates and onto the property. His contentment rubbed alongside pride as his luxury white home with its timber-louvred shutters open to the afternoon breeze came into view. He'd bought it several years ago as part of an ageing hotel. Then he had negotiated with the owners to bring the whole resort into the twenty-first century by becoming a silent partner.

It had been a gamble, sinking his first million into something he knew little about, but it had paid off, providing an ongoing income for locals. He hadn't done too badly out of it himself. He didn't get involved with the day-to-day business but he spent time at the resort when he wasn't working, knew the staff, attended festivities, checked on its overall efficiency.

But his private home was a sanctuary he guarded fiercely with high walls and monitored security. He didn't entertain here and no woman ever came within these walls. Not since Angelica. If he wanted female company while he was in Fiji, he found it elsewhere at another resort, preferably away from the main island.

The car stopped and Nic stepped out, leaving Malakai to park it undercover and bring in his luggage as he always insisted on doing as part of his job.

Luxuriant foliage and tropical flowers lined the path. He noticed a couple of recently planted hibiscus bushes and one of Tenika's personal touches—a Fijian carving, the equivalent of a garden gnome.

Over the next few hours he caught up with Malakai and Tenika over refreshments, admired the new kitchen garden they'd planted in his absence.

Later, refreshed from a swim and a shower, he checked his computer. Twilight settled over the bay with purple and vermilion hues. The smell of the resort's kerosene torches wafted through the window. The nightly traditional *Meke* on the lawns down by the sea was in full swing. Distant singing and drumming throbbed on the air. Nic sat back, satisfied the five massive screens reflecting a three-dimensional wrap-around image of the Utopian world he'd created were ready to work on.

Utopian Twilight had been his first major success, written—inspired—after The Angelica Incident. It had taken three years in the courts to reclaim the earlier works she and her lover on the side had plagiarised. Retreating from real life's raw deal into his alternative world had saved him.

Chameleon Twilight had followed a couple of years later. *Chameleon Council*, the final in the trilogy, was almost finished. He needed a break to revitalise his creativity, but online gamers were clamouring for more of the Onyx One's adventures. So... Leaning back, he tapped his fingers on the edge of his desk... Bring in an unexpected new love interest for the Onyx to keep the female players on board...?

From his upstairs office window, his gaze drifted to the exclusive club bures. Maybe his last-minute heroine would be a woman with a quirky penchant for personalised accessories...with a mysterious past...

After checking in to the resort, dinner in her room and an early night, Charlotte spent the first day lazing by her pool and catching up on a novel she'd been meaning to read for ever. She also enjoyed the warm tropical air on her winter-pale skin, the wide blue Pacific view from her balcony, the friendly room service.

It was because she needed some alone time—not because she didn't want to bump into Nic.

In fact, she didn't think of Nic at all. And she did *not* look at that fifty-dollar note burning a hole at the bottom of her bag. It was illegal to deface money, wasn't it? She ought to report him.

He was reminding her that he was here somewhere. Available. A phone call away.

On the second morning she threw back the sheets at six a.m. She would not allow him to dictate what she could and could not do on her first precious vacation in more than two years. Why should she feel like a prisoner in such a luxurious resort with the balmy breeze tickling her skin and beckoning her outside for an early morning walk?

So after a quick breakfast in her room, she pulled on a pair of skinny white pants and a shell-pink T-shirt. She piled her pad and pencils and a bottle of water in her holdall, plonked her sunhat on her head and ventured out.

She breathed in the salty beach smell. Breakfast aromas from the open-air restaurant. Freedom and relaxation.

The thick, scented air stroked her skin as she set off past the bures and along tidy curved paths flanked with Fijian Fire Plants and their brilliant red and gold and chartreuse leaves.

She passed the early risers heading towards the pools and other water activities. She could hear the distant splashes and laughter over the soft murmur of the sea. It sounded like fun.

But, for today at least, she wanted alone time with no distractions. She headed for a clump of scraggy casuarinas and Screw Pines not far away.

Three weeks ago she'd sold her parents' winery where she'd always worked. It had been a close-knit family business and she'd managed the office. The new owners had invited her to stay on but she didn't want to work with strangers who might want to change the way her family had operated the business for generations.

She didn't need paid employment—she had her inheritance—but she had to do *something*. The charities she and her mum had put so many hours into weren't enough of a challenge or distraction.

Until she came up with that elusive something, she'd continue with her lingerie designs, which she'd played with over the past few years. Only a hobby, but she loved the whole process—the designing, the construction and, most of all, the wearing of them.

Underneath her plain outerwear, she could indulge her secret passion for sexy and be that sensual woman she wanted to be. The way Nic had made her feel for those few special hours…

Get that thought out of your head.

As she approached the pines she saw colourful bougainvillea trailing over a high cream wall. She noticed a wide break in the foliage and walked through. A bright umbrella provided shade for the wooden table and chairs. There were a couple of recliner chairs covered with striped matting for those who wanted to sunbathe, but it seemed the guests were more interested in the water because there wasn't a soul around. Perfect.

She opened her sketch pad and spread it on the table, pulled out her pencils and let her hand wander over the paper, experimenting.

The Pacific Islands. Vivid colours and bold designs. Sexy playful styles that spoke of fun and summer. But with her libido still so highly charged, she could still feel the sparks and her ideas soon turned to more erotic designs. Crotchless knickers. Hmm. They'd have come in handy the other night…

Her hand moved quicker over the paper as ideas formed. She'd just finished designing an idea for a bra with a starburst radiating from a peek-a-boo cut-out in the centre of the cups when she heard the sound of heavy footsteps approaching.

'Hey, there. You.' The deep male voice shattered the peace like a volley of gun shots. Stern, annoyed. And familiar. She jerked her hat lower, pushed her sunglasses further up her nose and peeked beneath the brim.

Nic was striding towards her in a pair of short white

shorts. The rest of him was naked, showing off his well-defined abs and a washboard stomach glistening in the sun. He'd been swimming or working out. More like swimming by the way his shorts clung to his thighs. Her breath caught and her pulse did a crazy happy dance.

She ordered it to *stop*. 'Are you stalking me? Bec—'

'Stalking *you*?' he snapped out. 'You're on private property.' He came to an abrupt halt a few metres away, squinting and shielding his eyes against the sun's early morning rays. 'Charlotte?'

Spreading her trembling hands over her sketches to hide them, she managed to flip the cover down and stood up to minimise the difference in height. 'I—'

'What are you doing here?'

'It's a free resort,' she said, lifting her chin. 'And what do you mean private property?' A not-so-funny feeling slid through her stomach... He'd not checked in to the resort with her... 'I had no idea this part was private property. What are *you*—?'

'The sign on the gate gave you no clue?'

'What gate?' She looked back to where she'd come from. 'Oh. That gate.' That big double gate with 'Private Property, No Guests' on it in big black letters. She swung to face him. 'If you leave it open so wide that no one knows it's there, one can't be blamed for not seeing it.'

He exhaled sharply and muttered, 'The furniture movers must have left it open.'

Mind brimming with questions, she stared at him, then at the surroundings. Her eyes flicked over his shoulder and now she noticed glimpses of a thatched structure—probably a pool shade—through the heavy bushes. 'You live here?'

He moved a step closer, his gaze curious and drawn to her sketch pad. 'What are you doing?'

'Nothing.' Snatching her pad off the table, she slapped it against her chest. 'Just sketching. The flowers. Leaves. Shapes. Nothing really.'

'How do I know?' His dark eyes captured hers. 'It could be *you* stalking *me*. I don't know you, after all, do I, Charlotte? How do I know you're not here to—?'

'Who *are* you?'

'Nic Russo. And I live here.' He gestured with his chin. 'Show me what you're working on.'

Sketches of scantily clad female anatomy? 'No. It's private.'

One brow lifted. 'So is this garden.'

'And it's beautiful.' She said the first thing that came into her spinning head. 'Stunning. And I love those masks on the wall...'

'So are you—beautiful and stunning.' His voice slid over her senses like honey. 'Are you wearing a mask too, Charlotte? Hiding who you really are?' He resumed walking towards her. Predatory male with his prey cornered.

She slid one foot ever-so-slightly backwards, mentally calculating the direction of the gate behind her. Trying to figure how long it would take to get there if she ran very fast. 'No. I'm a private person, that's all.'

'So am I when it comes to guarding what's mine. Maybe that reporter was onto something,' he continued slowly, as if enjoying himself. But she couldn't be sure. 'Maybe you're an undercover spy. Out to steal my next project.'

'*Spy?*' she sputtered, incredulous, but, for heaven's sake, now he looked *serious*. 'Steal?' She took another step back. 'Are you living in some alternate reality or just plain crazy?' She shook her head, kept walking backwards. 'I refuse to have this ridiculous conversation.'

He followed, quickly gaining on her. 'Alternate reality. Interesting you should say that. A coincidence?' He was so close now she could see his long black eyelashes. Every pinprick of dark stubble. The *almost* smile tucked away at the corner of his mouth. Maybe.

But maybe not.

'I apologise for trespassing,' she went on, 'but I'd appreciate a straight answer before I leave.'

'And if I give you that answer, will you let me see what you're working on?'

She tightened her grip on her work. 'No.'

He spread his hands. Resigned? Somehow she didn't think so. She tapped her finger against the pad. 'Straight answer, please.'

'I write computer programs. Very lucrative computer programs.'

'Oh…' She'd figured he was more of an outdoors job kind of guy. 'Like accounting software, that kind of stuff?'

'Not quite.' He sounded amused. 'Do I look like an accountant?'

She grinned, amused right back despite herself. 'Not quite.'

'I build alternative worlds and create characters to live there. It's interactive. Anyone can visit so long as they pay and log in online. But some people think it's okay to steal work that's taken another person years of blood, sweat and tears to write.' There was a cold, implacable calm of personal experience behind the brown gaze.

'Okay. I understand. I'm sorry, I just saw the garden and no one was around…'

'Or maybe you couldn't stay away.' His voice deepened, his eyes changed. Tempted. 'You asked about me around the resort and came to tell me you wanted to continue what we started for a few more days.'

'No…Nic…I…' *need to think*. Except she couldn't remember what about when he was looking at her that way.

He closed the gap between them. She could smell the sharpness of salt water on his hot masculine skin. 'No...'

The breeze had strengthened and his hair blew around his face as he said, 'You could clear everything up if you prove you're actually working on something here and not just lurking.'

'I wasn't lurking, I was—'

'Hoping desperately that I'd come out and find you,' he murmured silkily. She heard his words but it was their smooth, deep cadence that captured her. She remembered how it had sounded when he'd laid her down on the bed and told her what he was going to do to her, and how.

He took her hat off, tossed it on the table. His hands moulded firmly around her shoulders and he pulled her closer, his lips a warm whisper away from hers. She swayed towards them, couldn't wait to feel them on hers. When he pulled the pad out of her loosening grasp and laid it on the table beside her, she didn't attempt to stop him.

'Because if *I* found *you*,' he continued, 'you'd not be giving in first.' He tightened his hold, eyes dancing. 'And that's okay. I don't mind letting you win. This time.'

Before she could object to that—did she even care?— his mouth swooped on hers. Smoothly, expertly, confident that she couldn't resist.

Instant addiction. She felt herself being swept up in the tastes and sensations as a stiff breeze swept across her sweat-damp skin and rustled the palm fronds. Unable to stop herself, she slid her hands upwards over sun-warmed skin exploring all the different textures while his mouth worked magic on hers.

But if he was just proving a point and he'd meant it to be light and easy, the emotions rushing through her were anything but. Distant alarm bells rang a warning. She wasn't ready for these feelings and this thing with Nic would only end badly for her. She'd stop…any moment now…

The muscles in her legs turned lax, her arms coiled around his neck and she hung on, her toes curling inside her sandals.

Nic lifted his lips a fraction. 'I hate to interrupt this, but your work…'

'Work?' she murmured, craning her neck to recapture his lips.

He licked her bottom lip with a lazy stroke of his tongue. 'Whatever you were doing. When I interrupted you. Remember that private thing you didn't want me to see?'

She pulled back and swivelled her head to see her precious designs scattering like giant butterflies across the garden. 'Oh, no!' Yanking out of his arms, she stumbled across the lawn and into bushes, grabbing what she could. 'I've got them,' she yelled in case he followed. 'Do *not* look…'

But when she turned around with the crumpled pages in her hands, he was regarding her with telling interest. He didn't say a word but a smile played around his lips.

'I'm leaving now,' she told him, her face burning. Stuffing her papers and everything she could lay her hands on into her holdall, she grabbed her hat and backed towards the gate. 'Stay away from me. I mean it,' she said through clenched teeth when he only kept smiling that know-all smile. 'You're bad for me.'

She turned and fled, knowing he was watching. Bad for her peace of mind. Bad for her will power. Bad distraction.

Bad, bad, bad.

Still grinning, Nic watched her go. He waited until she'd disappeared past the gate, then retrieved a loose sheet that had snagged under the table. He couldn't *not* look, now, could he? Smoothing out the page, he stared at the erotic image.

Flowers, hmm? His grin broadened. But he looked closer. This was a skilled artist's work. She'd added notes on the construction, fabric details, colour combinations.

And his initial response to finding her in his garden had been to shoot first, ask questions later. Good God, he'd all but accused her of espionage. He hoped his quick manoeuvre to kiss her instead had distracted her thoughts elsewhere.

It sure as hell had distracted *him*.

He folded the paper in half. The perfect excuse to see her again. Not that he needed one. He closed and secured the gates, his thoughts filled with his unexpected visitor. Naturally she'd want her design back. It was only right that he returned it. Tonight was soon enough.

He went straight to his computer, sat down and studied the screens alive with characters going about their quests in their fantasy world. Tapping the mouse, he got back to work. He had a full day's adventures to finish before he could turn his thoughts to other pursuits.

Closing her door safely behind her, Charlotte shut her eyes. Images danced behind her eyelids. Images of losing control. *Hoping desperately that I'd come out and find you,* he'd said. Huh. Like he'd know. Except he did. And she couldn't fool herself—desperate was exactly how she felt, which was why she'd told him to stay away. The only sensible thing she'd said to him. And the bit about him being bad for her.

Because she knew his type—he could charm the knickers off a nun with a single tilt of those lips—and that wasn't the type of man she wanted to get involved with. Nic was a great—perfect—one-night kind of guy, but that kind wasn't the sort of man she wanted to share other things with. Like confidences and dreams and hopes and interests. Like building a life and a home together. Like sharing his family to help compensate for the loss of hers.

Nic was so not that man.

Crossing the room to gaze over the rooftops, she picked out his palatial two-storey home amongst the trees. 'Oh, Dad, what would you say about me?' After her behaviour, she was hardly his princess any more. Her fingers touched the pearls at her neck. Mum would be appalled.

Nic *Russo*… Turning away from the view, she opened her notebook PC and switched it on. Thirty seconds later she was looking up the name and checking the social-networking sites. But the Nic Russos she found on the Internet didn't match anyone who created computer games and obviously made millions doing so. Not even a Dominic Russo turned up anything.

Her fingers clenched over the keyboard. As soon as she'd calmed down, when her mind was less cluttered and she'd thought things through, she'd find Nic Russo or whoever the heck he was and demand more answers.

If he didn't find her first.

CHAPTER SIX

AT FIVE-THIRTY Nic showered and went downstairs, Charlotte's paper in his shirt pocket. Tenika had ironed him a Fijian shirt—crimson with a white hibiscus print—and laid it on his bed along with a fresh white hibiscus. He knew she expected to see him wearing both.

She was in the kitchen washing the vegetables he'd seen her pick earlier from his window. These days her wiry close-cropped hair was tinged with silver. The patterned hot-pink blouse over her black *sulu* complemented her dusky complexion; her hands were busy pulling leaves off stems.

He reached for a banana. 'How's your day been?'

She turned from the sink and smiled, teeth white against her skin. '*Bula*, Nic, you want *kakana* already? Eat vegetables today from the garden with fresh fish.'

'*Vinaka*, but don't cook anything for me this evening.'

'Ah, you have a pretty *marama* waiting for you.' She looked him up and down and nodded approvingly. '*Totoka*. Very handsome. She is lucky. A guest at the resort, Malakai told me.' Her eyes danced with matchmaking delight.

Nic had to smile. The pair of them never gave up no matter how often he told them he was more than happy with his bachelor status. 'Malakai's jumping to conclusions.'

She shook her head, put the leaves in a colander and turned on the tap. 'He doesn't jump—he is too old. He said you and the pretty *marama* were talking in the car yesterday. Very close.'

'Charlotte was on the same flight. I have something I need to return to her.'

Tenika made a *pfft* sound and sloshed water about in the sink. 'You like her—Charlotte. You want Malakai to bring the car around?'

'We're not leaving the resort. We're just going to watch the *Meke* then maybe have a meal.'

'You bring her here tomorrow so I can meet her and see for myself if she is good enough for you. I can cook good *kakana* for you and her.'

'I don't think so.'

She strained off the leaves, dumped them in a bowl. 'You never bring the pretty *maramas* here. To your home.' She pursed her lips, her coal-black eyes pierced his. 'Maybe you like this one more than the others—you bring her.'

'Tenika...'

'Maybe you marry her. Make babies.' Wiping her hands on her apron, she nodded to him. 'Fijian people like babies. I can help.'

Tenika and Malakai had never had children of their own. Nic saw the emptiness in her eyes sometimes but Tenika would have to look elsewhere for surrogate grandkids.

'I know you can,' he said softly. He took the hibiscus from behind his ear and slid it behind hers. 'I'll see you tomorrow.'

He took the back route through the gate to avoid running into staff who'd expect him to stop and talk. He'd planned his time and didn't want those plans disrupted. The *Meke* started at dusk. This evening was perfect—still and warm, with a multi-hued sky and the charcoal aroma from the open-air barbecue.

He had access to all areas of the complex and it had been a simple task to learn that she was staying in one of the resort's most exclusive bures.

He knocked, and a moment later she cracked open the door.

'Good evening.'

She opened the door wider. 'I've been expecting you to show up.' She wore a black sarong spattered with electric blue and white frangipani flowers, giving him an unobstructed view of her neck and shoulders—his gaze lowered—and obviously no bra. Her glossy hair was piled on top of her head.

'It was only a matter of time.' He leaned against the door frame with a smile.

'Guess you'd better come in.' She walked away but looked back at him over one of those bare shoulders. 'Did you work your charm on the girls at Reception too?'

He stepped inside, closed the door behind him. 'Didn't need to. I'm a silent partner—finding one Charlotte Dumont on the books was easy peasy.'

Her shoulders tensed before she continued across the room. 'I see.'

'Your name was on Malakai's airport's pick-up sheet.'

'And, of course, you couldn't help noticing.' Those pretty grey eyes were clouded with worry when she finally stopped and turned to him. 'So I guess you know all about me now.'

'If you mean did I do a computer check on you, the answer's no. I respect privacy. But if you want to tell me a bit about yourself, that's fine too. I was hoping it might be tonight.' He saw her notebook PC on the desk and gestured with his chin. 'You won't find me on any social-networking sites.'

She blushed. *Guilty.* 'I wasn't... Much.' She crossed to the desk quickly and switched it off. 'You said you write computer games. I'd've thought you'd want a link so your fans could contact you.'

'I use a pseudonym.'

'That's convenient.' Her tone was sceptical, like her expression.

'Isn't it.' Walking towards her, he dug his wallet from his back pocket and flashed his driver's licence in front of her eyes. 'Read this. Aloud.'

'Dominic T. Russo.' She nodded. 'Okay.'

'And...' he took out her sketch, unfolded it and held it out '...I thought you might be wondering where this was.'

She took one look at the page, closed her eyes and folded it again and muttered something short and unexpectedly earthy.

'Charlotte, you just keep on surprising me.' He loved the way her cheeks coloured, the vulnerability she couldn't hide. It stirred up his protective side, amongst other things. 'Your secrets are safe with me.'

Her eyes darkened and sparked at the same time and he knew she was thinking about their one night together. Her fingers tightened on the page. 'I didn't even check them... You flustered me this morning.' She fanned her face with it. 'You're flustering me now.'

'Am I?' He assumed an expression of mock concern. 'Anything I can do to help ease that?'

'I refuse to answer on the grounds that it might cause me to break out in a rash that would prohibit me from leaving this room for the rest of the evening.'

'Tell you what, why don't you answer and we'll deal with the rash together if it happens?'

'Why don't I?' But she only slid the page between the covers of her sketch pad. 'Thanks for hand-delivering it.'

'I didn't think you'd want it floating around the complex. It looks important,' he prompted.

But she only said, 'It could be,' without elaborating and slid her notebook into its leather bag. 'I was just going to change and go down to watch the dancing.'

'That's handy because I came to ask you if you'd like to accompany me and maybe get something to eat after. But don't change, you fit right in as you are. The resort's casual, and loads of tourists wear their swimming costumes and sarongs.'

'Not me.' She crossed to the cupboard, pulled out a long white dress.

He shook his head. As stunning as he imagined she'd look in the slim sheath, he wanted to see her in those vibrant colours for a change. They accentuated her eyes and made them come alive. 'When in the islands, do as the islanders do. Keep the sarong. Please.' Besides, he wanted the chance to take it off her later.

She drew in a deep breath as if giving it some thought, then slid the dress back in the cupboard and said, 'Give me a moment to freshen up at least,' and disappeared into the en-suite bathroom.

He sat on one of the roomy saucer-shaped bamboo chairs to wait. Her suitcase was open on the bag stand. His gaze wandered over the contents. Underwear. Every colour, every fabric, every fantasy. If he had his way, he'd enjoy watching her dance instead, wearing his choice of garments. Then peeling every one of them from her body. Slowly.

But he put those carnal thoughts on hold. Tonight was about getting to know her in a social context. It was about discovering more about Charlotte the person.

To start with, at least.

Walking to the window, he stared out at the sunset reflecting off the ocean. They'd get to know each other a little better, enjoy a few more nights together, then she'd be gone. He didn't even have to make some excuse to call it off and leave.

Perfect.

Charlotte's fingers trembled slightly as she pulled the elastic out of her hair. She ran a brush through the tangled mess. Seeing Nic hadn't made her shaky—if you discounted the quiver of desire running the length of her inner thighs the instant he'd appeared in her doorway—it was the knowledge that he'd seen her risqué bedroom designs.

She adjusted and retied the sarong's knot between her breasts. She hated drawing attention to herself but maybe Nic was right. If she went casual, she'd blend in with the rest of the crowd. She left her hair down, scooping one side behind her ear.

So much for telling Nic to stay away. She knew exactly how the evening was going to end if he had his way. And she wouldn't fight it; she knew that too.

She was also looking forward to watching the traditional dance with him, sharing some time over a drink or a meal. Finding answers. As long as she treated him with the caution one usually reserved for dangerous animals, she'd be fine.

It was a perfect outdoors evening. The still water reflected the last sliver of sun. Coconut palms were silhouetted against an ocean of red and an orange sky. Someone was lighting the kerosene torches and cauldrons; the warm smell wafted on the sultry air.

'The younger kids from the local village school are performing tonight,' he said as they walked towards the

sounds of tribal drumming. There was an almost posses-
sive note to his voice.

'You know these kids?'

'I've been involved with the school's computer literacy
programme for a couple of years now, so yeah. The older
kids help the younger ones. One big family, no one's excluded. It's the Fijian way.'

From his tone, Charlotte had a feeling Nic had missed
out on those things while growing up.

They sat on benches with other guests to watch the
show. A troupe of male dancers entertained them first, burnished bodies gleaming in the firelight. Then the women,
festooned with flowers, their grass skirts alive with movement. The kids joined in last, to the audience's delight and
applause.

As the crowd dispersed to find their way to one of the
complex's half a dozen restaurants, Nic signalled one of
the dancers. 'Kas!'

'Nic!' she called, with a smile, and hurried over, her grass
skirt rustling. '*Bula*. You're back!' They bussed cheeks. 'The
kids have missed you.' She tapped him lightly with her palm
fan. 'Hope you're going to remedy that soon.' She turned
her wide smile on Charlotte. '*Bula*.'

'Charlotte,' he said, with a light touch at her back. 'This
is Kasanita Blackman, our dance teacher—just one of her
many teaching skills. Charlotte's a friend visiting here for
a couple of weeks.'

'*Bula*. It's nice to meet you.'

'Welcome to Fiji, Charlotte. I hope you enjoyed our
special performance. We've been practising for a month.'

'It was fantastic. The kids seemed to be enjoying it as
much as the audience.'

'Ah, yes, they're so excited.' Kasanita groaned. 'I don't
think we'll get any serious school work done tomorrow.'

Charlotte grinned. 'I bet.'

'Why don't you come and visit us while you're here? Get Nic to bring you when he comes. That's assuming you like kids and noise.'

'I love kids and noise…I think. I haven't been inside a classroom in years.'

'Okay, then. I hope to see you soon. Nic?'

'How about tomorrow? Charlotte?' He turned to her. 'Does that suit you?'

She smiled. 'I'm looking forward to it already.'

A chance to see a little of the real Fiji that other tourists might not. But more than that, she was looking forward to learning more about Nic and the support he gave the school. She admired guys who supported charities, especially when there was nothing in it for them personally—unlike Flynn who only did it to further his political ambitions.

They chatted with Kasanita a few moments then said their goodbyes.

'She's lovely,' Charlotte said as they walked towards one of the outdoor restaurants. 'English surname—did she marry an Aussie?'

'Her father's Australian, her mother's a local. He came here for work, they met and he never left.'

He led her to a quiet candle-lit table away from the rest of the diners and she knew he'd reserved it for them in advance. Right on the sand with the water lapping a few metres away, spotlights throwing up an amber glow on coconut palms, a candle in a frosted glass on the table.

A waiter appeared, his black *sulu* topped with the resort's black and aqua shirt. He set a couple of fancy fruit cocktails in front of them. Nic ordered a shared plate of local Indian delicacies and spoke with Timi for a few moments—he seemed to be on a first-name basis with all the staff—then they toasted the evening with their drinks. Something deliciously smooth and frothy with coconut, pineapple, fresh lime and alcohol.

Nic waited until Timi had gone to get closer to his dinner companion. Her hands were resting on the table as she leaned back on her chair to admire the stars and he couldn't resist running a finger lightly across her knuckles.

'So, Charlotte,' he began, capturing her eyes as her gaze snapped back to him. 'We've seen each other naked. I think it's time we got acquainted on another level, don't you?'

She made some kind of strangled sound in her throat and sucked deeply on her cocktail straw. He'd never seen such beautiful eyes. Even in semi-darkness they shone with an inner luminescence that only drew him closer. *A moth to the flame*.

He leaned in, his forearms on the table. He didn't mind the heat, and he wasn't averse to taking a risk. Taking risks had got him where he was today, but he waited a moment longer to let her settle. 'Ask me something.'

'Okay, I have a question,' she said slowly. 'Kasanita mentioned you've not been back in a while, yet you said you live here—how does that work?'

'I have an apartment in Adelaide. I divide my time between the two.'

Her eyes flickered. 'You're from Adelaide too?'

'Originally from Victoria. I moved to South Australia more than ten years ago. So there's a possibility of seeing you wandering Adelaide's Rundle Mall some day?'

'I live in the Barossa Valley, but the mall's a favourite haunt, yes.'

'You're not related to Lance Dumont by any chance?' He was a society big name in South Australia and royalty in the wine industry. Dumont owned the award-winning Three Cockatoos Winery. The man was worth a fortune.

She nodded and her gaze dropped to the table. 'He was my father.'

'So you *are* a princess after all.' Then he remembered that Lance and his wife had died in an aviation accident some time back, and his casual grin vanished. 'Hell, Charlotte, I'm sorry... I didn't mean to bring up painful memories.'

'It's okay.' She looked up again with a watery sheen in her eyes and a determined brightness to her voice. 'It's been a couple of years now. But I do miss them. And Travers.'

'Travers?' A boyfriend? A *husband*?

'My brother. I lost my whole family in one crazy afternoon and my safe little world crashed as surely as that helicopter. It's never been the same since.'

'That's tough,' he murmured, and meant it. He didn't know how it felt to have a family—at least not a family where people loved and cared for each other—but he could empathise with those who did when he saw the pain of loss in their eyes. Even though he didn't need or want that connection himself. 'Do the authorities know what happened?'

'Dad had a heart attack at the controls. We had no idea he had heart problems; he was always so fit and full of life. Dad loved to play up to the media.' She smiled a small private and poignant smile that tugged at his heart. 'He'd have been chuffed that he made the front page of the newspapers in three states.'

Their platter came. Charlotte set her linen napkin beside her plate and they ate for a few moments while they enjoyed the flavours of the food.

'You must be used to the press, then,' Nic said, choosing a coconut-covered melon ball.

'I've always avoided it whenever possible.'

'Why was that idiot reporter giving you a hard time?'

'I…' She trailed off on a sigh, and studied her wine glass as she twirled its stem between her fingers.

'You should tell me about it. That way if it happens again—'

'If it happens again, you won't be there to rescue me.' She met his eyes with a fierce finality and he knew it was the simple truth. She was leaving in two weeks. He wasn't.

'My fiancé and I broke up six weeks ago. He's in the public eye. The guy was chasing the story behind it. I thought, stupidly, if I denied my identity he'd leave me alone.'

'Did you love him? The fiancé.' His question surprised him. The reason behind it and the knot that tightened around his heart in response surprised him more.

Of course she'd loved the man, he thought. He was beginning to understand Charlotte's close ties to family. And he comprehended something very clearly: when she committed to people—whether it was her family or a man—it would be for keeps. So he figured she hadn't broken it off; her ex had.

In any case, she sidestepped his question, asking one of her own. 'What about your family, Nic?'

He never talked about his background. And with someone like Charlotte Dumont, society princess? He might as well be from the other side of the universe. She'd planned to marry and no doubt start her own family; he was a confirmed bachelor who lived for his work. Lived *in* his work; in a world where he ruled absolutely. They'd never find common ground.

Except in bed.

And wasn't that all that really mattered here? 'No siblings,' he said. 'I never knew my dad. My mother died twelve years ago.' He set his fork down carefully and reached for his glass. 'That's about it.'

'No.' She hesitated before placing her hand over his, and her eyes filled with compassion. 'That's the short, sharp and shiny version you give to anyone who asks. But I'm not anyone and I'm here and I have all night…if you want to talk?'

'I don't want to talk.' He turned her hand over, linked it with his. Slid his fingers slowly between hers, letting the tension build, watching her eyes change from sympathetic to wide and aware. Taking the focus away from his past. 'Are you still hungry?'

Shaking her head, she slipped her napkin in her bag. 'If I was, you just made me forget.'

With any other woman, he'd have smiled at the ease with which she'd surrendered, but the feelings Charlotte invoked were suddenly too strong for such trivialities. He rose and pulled her up, saw an answering flash in her eyes and tightened his grip. 'What I *really* want to do is unwrap you, lie you down and make you forget you ever had a fiancé.'

CHAPTER SEVEN

LEAVING the lights and music and chatter behind, Charlotte half walked, half ran, her hand in Nic's, urgency rushing through her veins like a waterfall after rain. They headed for soft sand and cool shadows and the eternal shoosh of the sea. As soon as they reached the shoreline she kicked off her sandals, swiped them up, laughing like a crazy woman.

Maybe it had something to do with near hysteria and never having experienced such urgency with a man. Flynn had been her only lover and it had been nothing like this.

Nic glanced down at her but didn't loosen his hold. 'What's funny?'

'This.' She waved her sandals in the air. 'Not so much funny as unexpected. I feel like a different person, I keep expecting to wake up and…'

Her laughter died and she trailed off and looked at him as he slowed his steps. His jaw was clenched, eyes fierce. A strange tight feeling clenched around her heart. 'What?'

He didn't answer, just pulled her further along the beach. The instant they were hidden from public view, he stopped and yanked her to him with both arms, so that she was pressed flat against his chest. 'Charlotte, what you make me want to do to you,' he muttered. He loosened his hold but only so that he could mould his hands around her skull. His fingers twisted in her hair as he crashed his mouth down on hers.

Demanding, desperate. She tasted the richness of his lips and tongue, the darker flavour of his desire. His grinding need against her belly. He was not the casually suave and charming man to let a woman take the lead tonight. He was that dangerous animal she'd warned herself about.

And she abandoned her caution absolutely. Gave herself up to him without reservation or hesitation. Her senses were so attuned, she felt every tremor: his and hers. The soft skitter of night air over her arms, the cool sand squishing between her toes. The heat flowing between their tightly pressed bodies.

She heard the mutter of appreciation as he kissed her, his groan of reluctance as he pulled away. He dragged his fingers down through the length of her hair, then let it fall softly to her shoulders. 'You were made for the night, Charlotte. That hint of the mysterious about you that makes me want to discover your deepest secrets.' He looked down at her, eyes as dark as the ocean. 'Do you still want to be alone?'

She knew it couldn't last, but right now she felt as if she never wanted to be alone again. 'I'd rather be with you,' she said, and reached out her hand for his.

'Come on,' he said, tugging her forward again. They followed the curve of the beach in silence, starlight guiding them, creating silvery streaks across the shallow pools between the thin ribbons of sand. No words were necessary, both knew where they were headed.

His home came into view, blocking out a slab of the night sky; she recognised the louvred windows and the scrawny pines spearing skywards behind the stone wall.

But instead of heading towards it, he led her further along the beach and up where the sand was soft, and coastal bushes provided protection. The air was pungent with marine life and rotting leaves.

'Here,' he said. 'No one'll find us.' He sounded out of breath, as if he'd been running a marathon.

'You sure?' They were both breathless and it wasn't only the rush to get here.

'Sure I'm sure.' A thread of that familiar teasing tone wound through the urgency. 'The bushes are adequate cover.'

His fingers fumbled a bit as he untied the knot between her breasts and she plain forgot about whether they could be seen. The silky material slithered away, leaving her naked but for a pair of sheer black lace panties threaded with red satin ribbon...and two red bows covering her nipples.

'Man, you are something else.' Appreciation darkened his gaze, molten chocolate desire as it skimmed over her body. 'Wow.' He fingered the bows, peeled them off with care, exposing her taut nipples to the cool air.

'These are designed for moments like this,' she told him and took his hands, placed them on her hips where the side seams were held together with matching bows.

Humour touched his mouth. 'You're a clever girl.' He tugged on the ends of the ribbon, watched the panties fall apart. 'And a little bit wicked.'

She knew she surprised him, that he'd prejudged her, and took pleasure in the fact as she unbuttoned his shirt with quick fingers, then reached for the snap on his jeans. 'I'm not what you expected, am I?' she said between breaths, sliding her fingers between the denim band and hard masculine abdomen. 'I'm not what I expected either—not with you. You turn me into someone I hardly know.'

His seductive hands were busy too, and a moan caught

in her throat as he flicked his thumbs over her nipples, the electric charge zapping straight to her womb. 'I think it's you who's wicked, Dominic Russo.'

'I think you talk too much,' he muttered, and shut her up with a long, drugging kiss that turned her blood to quicksilver and left both of them speechless.

Her head spun with his taste and the hot, arousing scent of his skin. He'd reduced her body to a quivering mess of need. Any moment her knees would give way. She gave up on trying to undress him and lifted her now useless hands to clutch at the sides of his open shirt. 'Hurry.'

A glint of a smile in those dark, dark eyes, and the sharpness, the intensity, the confidence of a man who knew his own sexual power. 'You'll need to let go of my shirt.'

Ah. Her arms fell limply as he shrugged it off. Grabbing a condom from his pocket, he shoved his jeans down long powerful legs, kicked the denim out of the way.

And then they were both naked, the night's soft light bathing them in silver and black. The stars seemed to spin closer as he spread her sarong on the sand and tumbled her down with him.

He was hard as steel and inside her in seconds, mouth and hands greedy, devouring her demands as if they were his own. Just what she needed, fast and frantic and so, so hot.

Clever man. He knew just what she wanted. What she craved. Dizzy delight, unimaginable pleasure—they pounded through her system the way a storm surge crashed onto the beach, bringing her to peak and leaving her swamped and stunned and ravaged. Not in pain, but in breathless, glorious delirium.

No time to recover, he took her up again, driving her to the crest of the highest wave and over, then dragging her

under with him to some deep airless place where sanity
vanished and passion ruled.

Finally spent, she coasted with him into calmer, shal-
lower waters where touches grew languorous and kisses
turned lingering. Time now to drift like the tide and think
only of this moment and this man.

'You're not what I expected either,' she murmured a
few moments later. Or it could have been hours—time no
longer seemed relevant.

He shifted so that he could pull the ends of her sarong
around them. 'What *did* you expect?'

'Not this.' She snuggled closer as the cooler air wafted
over her skin. 'I didn't expect this. Us.' The instant the
word was out she knew she'd made a mistake.

'Us…' he said, carefully. 'Babe, I don't do "us". I'm not
that kind of guy; you should know that up front.'

He was blunt to the point of being curt but at least he
was honest and she knew exactly where she stood. Which
was where she told herself she wanted to be. Casual. No
disappointments. But she'd given him the clingy female
impression—a big no-no.

'I meant the "us" as in being together again here kind
of us.' Embarrassed, she struggled for words. 'After all, it
was only supposed to be one night.' She raised her head
and forced a casual smile. 'Don't get the wrong idea.'

But he had got the wrong idea because he didn't smile
back, just went very still and looked up at the sky.

He'd made it obvious he wasn't looking for anything
more than temporary. Neither was she. She couldn't. Not
now, not yet. Maybe not ever, because she suddenly didn't
want to imagine being with a man who wasn't Nic in this
way ever again.

And how self-destructive was that kind of thinking?

She let her head flop back too, beside his, and stared

skywards at the drifting stars. 'I'm leaving soon anyway so whatever we have is brief. If you still…' She trailed off. She had no idea where his thoughts were.

'Two weeks. My hours are flexible and you're on vacation. We could spend that time together, if you'd like.' His fingers touched hers but his gaze remained fixed on the stars. 'What do you say?'

'A holiday romance?' Could she do that? Could she be romantically involved with a man knowing there was an end point? She'd never had a fling…

'Why not?' He shifted closer. 'Perfect location for romance. A man who wants to please you when you want to be pleased and who'll leave you alone when you want space. It'll do you good.'

'You think so?'

'It'll do us both good. I'll be your part-time tour guide with benefits, you'll be my muse.'

'Part-time tour guide with benefits.' She turned her head to look at him. 'Does that sound romantic to you?'

He looked back at her and smiled, and all the stars seemed to fall into his eyes. 'Trust me, I can do romantic.'

She bet he could. Problem was, could she let him do romantic and walk away unscathed?

After he'd seen Charlotte safely to her room and made arrangements to collect her for their school visit in the morning, restlessness drove Nic onto the balcony with a can of beer. He ripped off the tab, chugged down half the contents while he watched a ship's winking lights skim the horizon.

Anywhere else, he'd have invited himself to a woman's room to spend what was left of the night with her, but he had to consider his position at Vaka Malua. Which was why he never got involved with the resort's guests. He knew Charlotte had expected him to bring her back here. He'd seen it in her eyes when, instead of taking the quick route to his gate, they'd retraced their steps along the beach.

Us. She'd coupled them together and it had triggered that familiar sensation that the walls were closing in around him. It spelled long-term and commitment.

Not for Nic Russo. And he believed in being upfront and open about it. No false expectations. He drank deeply, paced to the end of the balcony and back. At least he was honest and Charlotte said she admired that about him.

So a couple of weeks… Romantic didn't have to mean complicated. Hell, no. He knew what women liked and it was a matter of pride that he'd never left a lover unsatisfied. They always understood his rules going in and were only too happy to play the game his way.

Of course, there were those few who hadn't played by those rules; those who'd tried to insinuate themselves into his life with home-cooked meals and gifts and, sometimes, in desperation, tears. Nic was immune to those tricks.

But Charlotte was unlike any other lover. She was fun and witty and sensual, but she was *more*. More than the sexually vibrant woman she'd allowed him to see. He'd glimpsed an inherent shyness and insecurity she worked hard to hide. She'd just come out of a serious relationship, which made her vulnerable to no-strings guys like him.

She'd tried to get him to open up about his past. And she'd wanted to soothe. To share. To understand. And for one unguarded moment he'd found himself strangely tempted.

But there was that thorny issue of trust. The brilliant, beautiful and devious Angelica had taught him people weren't always as they seemed and his fingers tensed on the can.

Just because he and Charlotte had a deeper than usual

rapport going didn't mean he wanted to book the resort's wedding chapel. A couple of weeks would be enough of an indulgence before getting back to what he did best. Work.

Stretching out on the wicker sofa, he breathed in the garden's damp night fragrance and concentrated on the soothing sound of the sea and the evening breeze on his skin.

Maybe she wouldn't be sleeping yet either. He punched the sofa's cushion into shape behind his head. Maybe she'd be spread out on that big bed, those pearls around her throat, reliving their passion. Would she touch herself, remembering how he'd touched her...?

It was a long time before he slept.

CHAPTER EIGHT

CHARLOTTE inspected her holiday wardrobe the following morning. She didn't want to fade into the background today. She wanted to dress the way she was feeling—sunny and happy. She wanted to fit in with the island culture.

She wanted Nic to notice.

With an hour before she was due to meet him, she headed for the central facilities and shops. She chose half a dozen picture books and jumbo crayons for Kasanita's class. Then she tried on clothes, finally settling on a bright tropical print dress in lime and hot pink. It reminded her of the way Nic's eyes had all but set her sarong on fire last night. Before he'd taken it off her.

Not her usual choice, she thought, staring at her reflection back in her room. And she liked it: being someone different. Here in Fiji she didn't need to worry about being recognised. Here she wasn't a big name's daughter or a politician's partner. She could be herself. She wasn't entirely familiar with the freedom of anonymity. Feeling as if she were dancing on air, she reached for her hat.

She was walking along the cool elevated breezeway towards the concierge desk on her way to meet Nic when she saw him on the lawns below chatting with a couple of female staff members. She paused at the balustrade. He wore khaki shorts and a white T-shirt with a black turtle motif, his slightly dishevelled hair catching the breeze, his smile blinding, even at this distance.

Like Flynn, he was a people person, charm and charisma personified. Another pretty girl joined them. Nic hugged the new arrival's shoulders, she smiled back and said something and they all laughed. Unlike Flynn, he wasn't using his charm to further any agenda. It was professional courtesy and respect and friendly interest all the way. Also unlike Flynn, Nic made time for people because he genuinely cared about others. And he was utterly, utterly gorgeous with it.

Her heart squeezed tight, then seemed to detach from her body and took off on a journey of its own.

Oh, no. She rubbed a hand over her chest and mentally dragged her heart back where it belonged and waited the longest time for it to settle.

She was no expert on men. Apart from co-workers and a forgettable couple of adolescent crushes, her experience was limited to her father and brother who'd loved her and an ex-fiancé who had not. Falling for Nic wasn't an option. This was a holiday romance, nothing more.

She turned and continued towards the concierge desk at the end of the open-air structure, taking her time to feel the salty air drifting through the covered walkway while her pulse returned to normal.

A colourful array of beads caught her eye and she paused to talk to the local women who came in from the nearby village daily and sat in the shade, their handcrafts spread on tarpaulins in front of them.

By the time she'd chosen a bracelet of tiny lime green stones to match her dress, Nic was waiting, watching her as she approached. She felt as admired and breathless as she had last night.

'*Bula*, Charlotte.' He looked her up and down. 'Don't you look bright and cheerful today.'

'Thanks.' She smiled. 'I *feel* bright and cheerful.' She saw the appreciation in his dark eyes and was glad she'd decided to buy something different.

As they drove inland and away from the coast in his luxury car she asked Nic about the education system.

'Here they lack the funds for equipment Australian schools take for granted, particularly in the rural areas.'

'Tell me about this school we're visiting.'

Nic overtook an ancient, rusted pick-up truck overloaded with workers on their way to the sugar-cane fields. 'It caters for children from five to twelve years, with two classrooms, two teachers and sixty kids. Kasanita teaches the kids up to the age of eight.'

'So how do they afford computers?'

'They don't.' He slowed for a bus stopping to pick up passengers.

'Oh?' Of course. 'You donated them.'

He shrugged a shoulder. 'It's a good cause.'

She nodded. He was a *cause* man. She loved causes. So often she'd found it to be women who put in the time and effort. 'How often do you visit?'

'When I'm here, I try to make it every couple of weeks. Early intervention's important, so I spend most of that time with Kas's class.'

'How do you know Kas?'

'Her father owns a yachting business and takes charter cruises around some of the local islands. But we've not talked much about you yet.' He glanced at her; more specifically at her breasts. 'I take it you're a fashion designer.'

She ignored the heat his gaze invoked and tried not to think about the underwear she'd chosen specifically in the hope that at some stage he'd take it off her. 'No. That's just a hobby.'

'A hobby.' His tone suggested he thought she lived on her parents' wealth. 'What do you do, then?'

'I worked at the winery, in the office.'

'Not any more?'

'I sold the business three weeks ago, so I'm out of a job at the moment.'

He didn't reply and maybe she was being oversensitive but she got the feeling he thought she was satisfied with her unemployed status. She hastened to explain she wasn't some rich chick with nothing to do but take exotic vacations. 'My ex and I were going to open a cheese and wine cellar door place there until he changed his mind and decided to give politics a go. And now...'

She looked away, at the green mountains in the distance, and thought how far away her problems seemed on this island paradise. How she had so many things to tackle on her return. How unready she still was to tackle them. 'I decided I couldn't, not on my own.'

He was silent as they drove past fields of banana palms and more jungle. Charlotte watched blurred walls of creeping green vegetation skim by, corrugated iron structures and primitive thatched roofs.

Finally he said, 'You could turn your designs into a business if you wanted to; they're unique enough.'

'No.' Her designs were her private indulgence and a solitary pursuit. She'd given it a lot of thought since Flynn had left and decided she needed work that involved social interaction if she wanted to avoid becoming a total recluse. 'Something'll turn up.' The charities her mother and she supported could keep her busy in the meanwhile.

The school was part of a village, quaint and old and basic—a single louvred building painted bright blue with a maroon roof and a wide porch. The playground's grass surface was patchy and devoid of shade or equipment and adjoined the ubiquitous village rugby field.

But it didn't lack vitality because the moment they pulled up at the door the children spilled outside, Kas following, and suddenly the car was surrounded with friendly faces.

'Bula! Bula!' The kids swarmed around them, hands on the car's windows, their laughs loud and happy.

She and Nic climbed out into humidity and hot sun, crushingly different from the car's air conditioning. A couple of chooks scratched at the ground and unfamiliar bird calls echoed in the trees.

Kasanita welcomed them. '*Bula*, Charlotte, Nic.'

After being presented with garlands of kid-made paper flowers, shells and bits of silver paper, they followed the noisy class inside like a couple of royal visitors. Children's colourful artwork more than made up for the room's sparse aspect, with one exception—the six computers along one wall.

Kas offered them fresh coconut milk, then quietened the children with her guitar. Charlotte and Nic sat on rush matting amongst the children and joined in. An interactive time followed, the children free to choose activities and show off their learning to their special visitors. There was an encore of the previous night's dance.

The visit gave Charlotte a further insight into Nic. He interacted with the children naturally and knew how to reach them on their level, whether it was explaining how to use a computer program or sharing a joke or peeling a tiny girl's banana.

'What do you say to fresh grilled fish for lunch?' Nic asked as they drove away, heading towards the coast once more. 'I know this little place.'

'Yes, please. I'm starving.'

'Did you enjoy yourself?'

'I loved it. Thanks for inviting me along.' So much sharing and caring and learning in such basic conditions was a contrast to her own privileged upbringing. 'The playground could do with some climbing equipment. Maybe some shade sails.' She turned to Nic. 'I'd like to help.'

He glanced her way. 'How do you mean?'

'Funding. One thing I do know is how to raise money.'

He looked at her a moment, eyes unreadable, then back at the road. 'You're not what I expected, Charlotte Dumont.'

She stiffened, staring back. 'Reverse snobbery, Nic? You think because I was born into a privileged family that I don't see what goes on around me? That I don't care? You're a self-made man,' she said slowly. 'What happened in your past that makes you think I'm less because my wealth came to me naturally?'

He shook his head, clearly unwilling or unable to talk about that past. 'You're being overly sensitive, Charlotte. I don't think that at all.'

She remembered the darkness in his eyes when she'd asked why he'd rescued her from that reporter. He had a deep-seated animosity towards bullies. Had someone treated him as less because he came from an impoverished background? He gave her nothing with which to draw any conclusions.

She didn't ask. Some secrets were best left undisclosed, especially with someone who was a temporary figure in her life.

'Maybe a fashion show,' she said a few moments later. 'My best friend has her own bridalwear business. Or I could model my lingerie,' she joked, to clear the air of residual tension that had sprung up.

Nic grinned, his fingers tightening on the wheel at the thousand and one images that stole like seduction into his mind's eye. 'Count me in.'

'I was kidding, Nic. As if that's going to happen,' she muttered.

'Why not?'

'Forget it.' Her voice lost its humour.

'No can do. I've got the image in my head now.' He turned off the main road. 'So I insist you model some of your creations for me this afternoon. A private showing.'

From the corner of his eye, he saw her hug her arms across her chest. 'Putting myself on display for a roomful of people is just not me, no matter what I'm wearing.'

'I'm not a roomful of people,' he said, looking at her briefly before turning his eyes back to the road.

She was staring at him behind her sunglasses. 'I'm not even sure I can do it for you.'

'Sure you can. Remember Melbourne?' He could. His groin tightened at the memory of her mindless abandonment.

She made a noise that could have been amusement or it could have been pain.

'You can let yourself go when you want to.'

'Maybe I'm afraid to,' she said quietly as he pulled up at 'Inoke's Catch of the Bay', one of his favourite out-of-the-way places. 'Maybe I'm afraid of this new person.'

'Don't be,' he said, just as quietly. He killed the engine and turned to her. He reached out to take off her glasses so he could see the silvery flecks in her wide, wide eyes. The bright tones of her new dress highlighted the light tan of her skin and lent colour to her cheeks. 'I like this person. I like her a lot.'

Her eyes remained huge and she chewed on her lower lip. 'And maybe I'm afraid of that too.'

Her words eerily echoed his own thoughts. 'It's okay, babe,' he said, as much for himself as for her. 'You don't have to change.' He combed his fingers through her hair, traced the fine curve of her jaw. 'But explore another side of yourself and you may find you like what you discover. Maybe it'll help you look at life differently when you go home.'

She nodded slowly. 'Maybe.' She seemed to shiver, then came out of her pensive mood as if by sheer determination and opened the car door. 'That's a lot of maybes.' She breathed deeply, the rich aroma of the grill wafting in. 'I'm starving.'

It was perfect—the food, the warm overcast weather, her company. They spent a leisurely hour eating, then Charlotte excused herself to freshen up in the restroom outside while he paid the bill. He spent a few moments chatting to the owner, a friend, Inoke, then spotted Charlotte further up the beach collecting shells that littered the bay's coarse sand.

He headed after her, admiring the carefree way she moved, long legs flashing in the sun. Her hair was tucked up under her hat. Those creamy shoulders were going to burn. Should've brought sunscreen, he thought, but his attention was snagged by a man approaching her.

Damn. As Nic picked up his pace he watched Charlotte stop and speak with the reporter—what else could he be with that long-range camera slung around his scrawny neck? Too far away to hear what they were saying. Sensing Nic's evil eye spearing his way, the reporter glanced towards Nic, then began retracing his steps to the car park. Nic changed direction.

'Hey, you!' Nic skidded to a halt in front of him, his feet throwing up sand, and glaring at the jerk through narrowed eyes. 'If I see you anywhere near her again, I'll sue you for harassment.' Tension simmered along his jaw and he spoke through clenched teeth. 'I might sue you anyway, just for the hell of it.'

'Hey, man, what's your damn problem?' The scrawny-necked reporter glared back. 'Ms Dumont's public property—' he looked closer '—*Mr* Russo. And I never forget a face.'

'Right back at you, mate. She's on a private vacation so back off or you'll have me to deal with.'

The man's eyes sparked with interest as they flitted towards Charlotte, then Nic. 'Private, eh?'

'Yeah, private; so get lost.'

'Like that lover of yours a few years back? What was her name?' He smiled—unpleasantly. 'Never pays to be on the wrong side of the press, *Mr* Russo.' Skirting Nic, he resumed walking.

Nic waited until the reporter climbed into his car and drove off before turning his attention to Charlotte, who hadn't moved from her spot and was watching on, her expression serious.

'You okay?' he said as he approached her. Concern slid through him. He shouldn't have goaded the man; he didn't want his threat to impact on Charlotte.

'Fine. He was harmless, Nic.' She shrugged, then smiled. 'Seems I can't avoid the press here after all.'

'What did he ask you?' he demanded. 'What did you tell him?'

'That I was enjoying Fiji very much.'

She ran a finger over the smooth shell she was holding then looked up at him from beneath the hat's brim. Even from behind her sunglasses her eyes shone, telling him he had a lot to do with how much she was enjoying her vacation.

'Thank you, but you don't have to fight my battles for me. I'm okay.'

From out of nowhere, a sense of possessiveness rose up inside him like a rogue wave—and everyone knew rogue waves were dangerous. 'Let's go, babe.' Shaking off the unnerving sensation, he grabbed her hand and started jogging back up the beach.

'Hang on.' She stumbled a little as he tugged her with him towards the car park. 'What's the sudden rush? The guy's gone; you scared him off good and proper.'

'You promised to model for me. I want to make sure you don't change your mind.'

'I never said…'

He turned and grinned at her. 'And in return, I promise you'll enjoy it as much as I will.'

'Oh.' She smiled back. 'Okay, when you put it like that what are we waiting for?'

They ran all the way back to the car.

'What shall I start with?' she said when they closed the door to her room behind them.

'Surprise me,' Nic said, tossing his sunglasses on the bed.

'But I don't know what you like.'

He touched his lips to hers, but didn't linger; he wanted to watch her show off her work first and draw out the anticipation. 'I guarantee I'll like anything you want to show me.' He helped himself to a bottle of water from the mini-fridge, poured half into a glass for Charlotte and set it on the shelf. 'Any colour that's not beige.'

'I don't have beige lingerie.'

'Thank God for that.' He took a long swig from the bottle.

'But I do have skin tone.'

'No skin tone. The only skin tone I want to see you in is the real thing. You're a girl who should breathe colour.'

'Okay, I'll start with what I'm wearing now.'

He didn't look at her as he walked to the louvred panel that closed off her balcony, slid it open. 'When you're ready, come out here.' Moist tropical air wafted in, scented with salt and foliage. The bure was perched on the hill, the balcony private and overlooking the sea. He stripped down to skin and set his clothes within reach on the edge of the pool.

The palms cast dappled shade on the water as he lowered himself into the pool and leaned back against the edge, spreading his arms along the tiles. He needed the water's bite to cool his blood and lend him restraint if he wasn't going to drag her in with him straight off and have his way with her.

To his relief, he didn't have long to wait.

She appeared in the doorway like a fantasy come to life and he quickly realised it wasn't relief, it was a form of torture. And he'd been the one to suggest it.

He held his breath, then let it out with a growl at the back of his throat as he took in the sight of her breasts spilling over a slash of hot pink and brilliant aqua. A tiny glimpse of dark nipple in the slit where pink met blue. The panties were kept together at the back with a cheeky blue shoelace.

'You were wearing *that* while we were in a classroom full of children?'

'Um…' She grinned, lips pressed together. 'Just lucky it wasn't gym class while we were there, wasn't it?'

He swallowed. 'I'm glad I didn't know. So that's your usual day wear?'

'Yes.' She ran the tips of her fingers inside the waistband of her panties. 'These are new. I've been working on a different line since I became single again. It's fun.'

'I'm sure it is…' He surged forward. 'Come here.'

With a mock stern look, she held up a finger. 'Not yet. This was your idea, remember.'

'Okay.' He just might last a few more moments, he thought as she disappeared again, leaving her tempting fragrance behind her. Then again, he might not.

Less than a minute later she was back in a black and white number. A skinny white lace thong. The string of black pearls at the back disappeared between firm, round buttocks.

His mouth watered and his eyes followed her as she circled the pool, keeping just out of reach. 'You're a naughty girl.'

She laughed lightly, her hands clasped behind her back, which had the arousing effect of pushing her breasts forward. Her nipples stood erect against the black lace like bullets. 'And the best part is that no one knows.'

'*I* know.'

'In which case, I may just have to kill you.' She crouched down, swished a hand through the water. 'But before I do, I think you'll like my wet look. Shiny black—'

'Come here.'

'Or my lotus butterfly…'

Frustration gave him agility and he surged forward, grasped a slender ankle. 'Later,' he told her, his hand moving higher, over her calf where her skin was hot and smooth and firm.

'But I'm just getting started,' the voice above him complained. 'And I've never done this before. Indulge me.'

He looked up, past lace and curves and bare flesh. Her eyes reflected the water's ripples, making them dance and sparkle with light and fun. She knew exactly what she was doing to him.

'Oh, I'll indulge you,' he promised, every cell in his body on fire. 'In the water. Now.'

'Oh, well, if you insist. But first, we need…' reaching for his trousers on the tiles beside him, she felt in the pockets and pulled out a foil packet '…one of these.'

With the condom packet between her teeth, she slid slowly down into the water beside him, inch by excruciating inch, the bra's lacy texture rasping against his chest. Her legs twined around his like electric eels, sending sparks shocking straight to his groin.

Fire and ice. Cool water swirling over hot skin. He slid his hand between her shoulder blades and down, over each vertebra, the pearls between her buttocks. Then he turned her around so that he could feel the erotic sensation of the tiny baubles against his erection. Groaning with the pleasure, he bit into her shoulder as he slid the lacy garment down her thighs with his hands, then his toes.

She tasted of the beach and the sun and freedom. 'You're gorgeous.' He unclasped her bra, then pulled her back against him and filled his hands with her womanly shape, feeling the tight, water-chilled buds against his fingers. 'Refreshing and gorgeous.'

Leaning back against him, she let her legs float to the surface in front of her. 'You're not half bad yourself.'

It was a languid moment at odds with the way his body craved and his mind reeled—because it wasn't just the physical intimacy he whispered about against her ear. He wanted more, and he wanted to tell her. How she blew him away on so many levels. How he'd never met anyone like her. So it was as well she broke the calm with a quick fluid movement.

When she turned to face him, he saw the same emotions in her eyes before she blinked them away with a sparkling smile.

'That's enough,' she said with a laugh. She dangled the foil packet above her head. 'You have to work for the rest.' Jerking out of his grasp, she ducked beneath the surface and shot away like a fair-skinned dolphin to the far end of the pool, elegant and sleek. Then she dived deeper and only her legs broke the surface, perfectly shaped calves, feet arched, toes pointed like a ballet dancer's.

Seconds later, she reappeared, swiped her hair from her face and waved the packet in front of her. 'Hey, you're supposed to come and catch me.'

'Where did you learn to swim like that?'

'Synchronised swimming classes at school for a couple of years.'

'Is harp playing on your list of accomplishments too?'

'Piano.'

He nodded. Naturally she'd have gone to a private and exclusive school, he thought, watching her careless smile. Taking such extra-curricular activities for granted. A school with its own private and exclusive pool. Halls of learning, where that learning was valued. The best education money could buy for the Barossa wine princess.

He thought of the school he'd attended in one of Melbourne's seedier districts. Neglected buildings. A cramped, pot-holed playground where kids were bored and turned their attention to other activities. Like making life a living hell for those younger and smaller than themselves.

She stared at him, her smile fading. 'Something wrong?'

He shook off the old taunts with a grin. 'What's wrong is you're too far away.' Then he dived under the water towards her.

CHAPTER NINE

SHIVERS chased over Charlotte's skin as Nic closed in, his tanned, muscled torso streamlined and swift. He seemed so predatory that instinctively she backed up, bumping against the pool's smooth tiles.

He surfaced right in front of her, water sluicing off his face and hair. 'Gotcha,' he murmured, snatching the forgotten condom from her nerveless fingers, then placing his arms on the pool's rim on either side of her.

Trapped. And right where she wanted to be.

Her breath caught in her throat. Her heart pounded. His eyes had lost the sombre expression she'd noticed seconds ago but what she saw there now was no less acute. Desire and intent. His gaze didn't leave hers as he ripped open the foil packet and sheathed himself.

Gone was the light-hearted banter, the teasing, the sexy foreplay. Something deeper emerged, like fresh water from a hidden spring. Mystifying and mysterious. As they watched each other an unspoken intimacy surrounded them like the heavy scent of the tropical blooms off the balcony.

She could hear the sounds of children splashing in the resort's family pool some distance away, the palm fronds flapping in the afternoon breeze. Nic's breathing. Her own. She was falling for him the way she'd never fallen for anyone before. Because he was unlike anyone she'd ever known.

And he wasn't the kind of guy she should be falling for. She needed stability, someone who'd be there for life. But she was powerless to resist him as he slid his hands over her breasts.

'Nic...'

'Shh.'

The heat of his tongue combined with the cool water, a mingling of stunning sensations as she leaned back on the edge of the pool, gave up trying to reason it all out and surrendered.

After the poolside chase and inevitable capture, she'd expected a fast and furious encounter, but this was lazy, almost luxurious. The long, slow pull of his mouth on her nipple. The glide of her legs between his. The sluggish swirl of water as he pushed slowly and deeply inside her.

Moaning with the pleasure, she slid her hands over his damp, water-cooled back, then across his shoulders, loving the hardness of him, her movements in slow motion while her mind drifted like organza ribbons in an idle draught.

He withdrew a little and raised his head to look at her. Then plunged deep and slow and true, filling her. *Ful*filling her.

Through heavy-lidded eyes, she watched him. The afternoon sun danced through the leaves and stroked his face with bronze. Luxuriant black lashes framed his eyes; hues of amber gleamed in the ebony irises. Once again she was the prey and she couldn't look away. Powerful, penetrating, persuasive, he drew her inside him until she no longer existed outside his aura. And the deep, dark places in her soul brimmed and overflowed with the emotion she was coming to realise only he could wring from her.

* * *

The days passed too swiftly. Nic took Charlotte on a yachting expedition to a nearby island where they enjoyed seafood and champagne on board, then went snorkelling in the aquamarine shallows and lazed on the golden beach. There were a couple of occasions when she felt the paparazzi's presence but they didn't approach and she didn't let it bother her. She loved the open-air farmers' markets alive with aromatic spices, greens of every description, pineapples, taro and yams.

They attended the resort's traditional *lovo* and kava ceremony. A whole pig, wrapped in palm leaves and surrounded with taro and breadfruit, was cooked in an earth oven filled with hot volcanic rocks. They enjoyed every sunset together. Whether it was sipping cocktails from one of the resort's restaurants, or making love on the private strip of beach near his house or enjoying a barbecue on board a schooner, Nic made every occasion unique.

She discovered new things about him. He liked having his ear lobes rubbed but vehemently refused to submit to the silk scarf blindfold she'd teased him with. There was a scar over his left hip from a surfing accident.

He sent fresh frangipanis to her room every day, took her on a midnight picnic, organised a candle-lit massage for the two of them on the beach and made love to her as if she were the only woman in the world, tenderly and fiercely and everything in between.

He couldn't have done much work unless he was a freak of nature and didn't require sleep. But he didn't sleep with her. Each night he returned to his house on the hill. She believed it was his way of maintaining that one-step-back rule he had.

He'd been straight with her from the start—*part-time tour guide with benefits*—giving her no reason to build a fantasy future around them. But it didn't stop her from lying awake at night by herself and imagining.

She wasn't a good muse after all. Nic leaned back in his chair, scowling at his computer screens. Stupid o'clock in the morning and nothing he tried was working. Every time he thought he knew where the game was heading, he hit a dead end. Charlotte—*Reena*, he corrected himself—his game's new heroine, blocked Onyx One's movements at every turn. Tugging at Onyx with her bewitching eyes and throwing him off balance. Charlotte's eyes.

Ridiculous. He forced the notion away, re-evaluated his last idea, then deleted it. He'd hit a snag, that was all. Just because his hero refused to cooperate and the plot wasn't panning out the way it should, didn't mean Charlotte had anything to do with it.

Or did it?

He swung his chair around and stared through the open doors where starlight painted the palms with silver. Maybe he should make the dark-haired Reena a blonde. Or a fiery redhead. Even a silver-haired temptress. But then, why allow his obsession with a woman to dictate the most important thing in his life—his work?

He'd end this thing with Charlotte now, and reclaim his creativity, which had mysteriously dried up. Shoving a hand through his hair, he glared at his screens. His modus operandi with women had been the same for years. Enjoy the fun and romance of it all but never let them too close. Never allow himself to forget Angelica and the lesson he'd learned. Work was his life, he didn't need anything or anyone.

But for the first time in for ever, his cyber world wasn't doing it for him. He wanted to spend what was left of Charlotte's time here with her. Preferably in bed.

He assured himself that, like all good endings, their

final goodbye should be a satisfying resolution. Then he'd be able to put it behind him and get on with what mattered in his life.

And what the hell was it about his predictable life that mattered so damn much? On an oath, he shut down his computer and paced to the window to stare at the black-roofed bures. White ribbons streaked the dark sea beyond, its gentle omnipresent sound soothing.

It wasn't only Charlotte's sensuality that had him burning and reaching for her over and over again. Beneath the hot-blooded goddess she had a vulnerability that tugged at his heart and made him want to protect her while at the same time coax her out of that shell he'd glimpsed when she thought he wasn't looking.

With Charlotte there was empathy—for himself and for others, both in her words and her actions. She had a wicked sense of humour he suspected she rarely allowed others to see. Deep down she was a private person, and, more, she recognised and *respected* that facet of his own personality.

Charlotte had made him realise that not all women were like Angelica, out to get whatever they could. He'd found a woman he not only enjoyed physically and socially, but one he could trust enough to allow a glimpse into his world, and tonight was his last chance to invite her into his home.

The next morning, instead of the usual bouquet of frangipani Charlotte had come to expect, a single white orchid arrived in a vase along with a gilt-edged envelope.

Her whole body turned to stone. Flynn had sent her a single white rose the morning after he'd ended their engagement. There'd been a little envelope and, inside, a card that said, 'Thanks for the memories.'

Palms sweating so hard she thought she'd drop the vase, she carried it outside to the table on the balcony and sat down. She stared at it for a long moment, a giant fist clenched around her heart. No matter what the message said, this was a timely reminder that her holiday fling with Nic was almost over.

She was still staring at it when Nic's special knock sounded on the door. Bracing herself, she went to open it.

He looked as fresh as the morning's orchid. As sexy as midnight on black silk sheets. 'Hi.' She gave him a smile and struggled to keep her voice free and easy while that fist tightened around her heart. 'Come on in. I'm nearly ready.'

He waited until she'd shut the door before kissing her thoroughly. She clung to him a moment before reminding herself she'd be gone in twenty-four hours, and deliberately stepped away first.

She swung away from the gorgeous sight of his well-honed body and walked to the balcony. 'The orchid's beautiful, thank you.'

'I saw it by the back door and thought of you.'

'You grow orchids?' She turned back to study him, head to one side. 'You just don't look the domestic gardening type.'

'Malakai does most of the work, actually.' He jiggled his brows. 'Want to come up and see my collection?'

A grin tugged at her mouth. 'Don't you mean Malakai's collection?'

'Whatever gets you there,' he said with an answering grin.

Surprise lifted her brows. 'To your house?'

Still grinning, he walked towards her. 'So you haven't read the note yet.'

'I haven't got around to it.' She hugged her arms, then recognised her insecure action and reached for the unopened envelope on the table. 'Actually, I was thinking of giving the market a miss this morning. I need some time...

To pack.' She stared at the table, preferring the orchid's beauty to the look she'd see in his eyes. The look that made her as helpless as a butterfly under glass.

'Fine.' He was suddenly there beside her, smelling of his familiar spicy cologne. He touched the side of her face. 'It's fine if that's true. But I know you better than you think. Something's changed.'

'Nothing's changed.'

'We've always been up front with each other, Charlotte. At least, I have.'

She bit down on her lip before deciding maybe it was time to give a little. After all, what did it matter now? 'It's weird, the timing—Flynn left me a white rose and a note when we…when *he* chose his career in politics over me.'

He studied her through narrowed eyes. 'Why did he have to choose? Why couldn't he have both?'

'Because I was an embarrassment to him. A liability for any potential politician.'

His brows lowered and his voice was hard as nails when he said, 'Then he's an idiot and you're better off without him.'

'Forget him. I have. The whole thing's a reminder to me that I'm leaving tomorrow.' *And you said it yourself, there is no 'us'.*

'So…have you got plans for when you get home?'

'I have tickets for the opera at the Festival Theatre to look forward to. It's "Carmen", my favourite.' Even if she'd more than likely bump into the press, who'd ask her all about the break-up.

But over the past couple of weeks her confidence had lifted. She'd not even felt out of her depth when the guy on the beach had approached her. Just a brief friendly exchange. Nothing to be alarmed about. She realised maybe she could—no, she *would*—face the public without the old insecurities.

'Tickets?' he was saying, dragging her back to the present. 'As in more than one?'

'Flynn was supposed to go with me. I bought them months ago. Do you like opera?'

'Never been.'

She nodded. 'It's not for everyone.'

His jaw tightened and she knew she'd offended him. That he thought she thought he wasn't cultured enough. Whatever the heck that meant.

She smiled to dispel an awkward moment and told him, 'It wasn't Dad's cup of tea either. Wild horses wouldn't have dragged him there.' She slid the envelope back and forth between her fingers. 'You'll be glad to get back to work, I bet. You've been neglecting it to entertain me.'

'It's been worth every moment.'

His eyes seemed to melt into hers and for an instant something dangerously like hope rose up inside her. Futile hope.

Then he swiped the envelope from her hand and screwed it up. 'Bad idea, this,' he said, tossing it into the waste-paper basket. 'So I'll just say it instead. I want you to join me for a popular Fijian meal tonight. And I'm going to cook.' He grabbed her hand and began tugging her to the door. 'Which is why we're going to the market.'

She tried to grab her bag on the fly. 'Hang on...'

He stopped and his eyes searched hers. 'Unless you really do want to be alone?'

No. She saw something in his brown-eyed gaze that had her heart stuttering. She picked up her bag and a hat. 'I'll pack this afternoon.'

Nic's waterfront home was airy and spacious, with white marbled floors and panoramic views of the coastline.

They'd barely set foot in the modern kitchen—vibrant red with stainless-steel appliances—when Nic's housekeeper appeared in the doorway with a wide flat basket of fresh-picked vegetables under one arm.

'Ah, there you are.' Nic smiled at the middle-aged woman. 'Tenika, I'd like you to meet Charlotte. Tenika's agreed to let me loose in the kitchen this evening.'

Charlotte nodded. '*Bula*. It's a pleasure to meet you, Tenika.'

'*Bula vinaka.*' Tenika's deep voice seemed to resonate through her ample body, her eyes livened with interest as they flicked between the two of them.

Nic's mobile rang at that moment and he excused himself and moved away to answer it.

'So how long have you worked for Nic?' Charlotte asked.

'Seven years. When he come here, he give me and my husband work. Very kind man.' She set her basket on the black granite counter top, nimble fingers picking off the few wilted leaves. 'You like Fiji?'

'Very much.'

'You come back again. Nic alone too much after that bad one gone.' She tossed the discarded leaves into the sink, the action as eloquent as any words.

'Bad one?' Charlotte's curiosity soared.

'Angelica,' Tenika muttered. 'Bad.'

Charlotte was dying to ask more but Nic was already ending his call.

Tenika lifted a couple of ripe mangoes from the bottom of her basket and turned on the tap. '*Ni mataka*, you go back to Australia?'

'Tomorrow, yes.'

'You and he had a friendly visit here, *io*?'

Nic exchanged an intimate glance with Charlotte that told her exactly how friendly her visit had been.

Charlotte was so caught up with watching Nic and controlling the sudden heat rushing up her neck, she barely noticed Tenika walk to the door.

'You come back again soon,' she said, smiling at the pair of them. 'I go now. Enjoy *kakana* together. *Moce*.'

'*Moce*. Goodnight.' Charlotte and Nic spoke in unison.

'Friendly, huh?' Charlotte said, slinging an arm around his neck as soon as they were alone. 'I assume *kakana* means a meal and not hot sex?'

Grinning, Nic gave her a casual kiss, then moved to the fridge and began taking out ingredients. A large fillet of fish, a plate of chopped cherry tomatoes and onions, a bowl of coconut milk. 'With Tenika, I wouldn't be too sure. Fijian women are born matchmakers.'

Best to leave that one alone. 'Anything I can do to help?'

'You can slice this lime if you want.' He set it in front of her with a knife.

Charlotte settled herself on a bar stool across from him. 'What are you cooking?'

'Fish in coconut milk. A special Fijian dish.' He sliced the fish into steaks. 'This is *paka paka*—fresh snapper.'

He set the pieces sizzling in a pan, then arranged the spinach and ginger leaves Tenika had picked on aluminium foil on a shallow dish and added the tomatoes and onion. The sharp, piquant aromas filled the kitchen.

'Taste this.' He dipped a spoon in the coconut milk and held it out. 'Freshly squeezed.'

'Oh, my.' She licked the thick substance from her lips while Nic placed the seared fish on the bed of leaves. 'That is rich, rich, rich.'

'Now we pour it over and add your lime.'

While Charlotte arranged the slices, she imagined how

it could be—the intimacy of being a couple and sharing the ups and downs of their day while they cooked the evening meal together.

But Nic wasn't that man and her heart faltered. What was she doing, thinking those thoughts? He was never going to offer any woman commitment. Was the woman called Angelica the reason?

'We seal the foil and let it bake while we drink cocktails and I give you the grand tour... What is it?'

She pulled herself back and realised he was watching her, a groove between his brows.

'Just thinking how much I'm going to miss...' *you* '...being here.'

'That's good to hear because it means I've been successful in my job as tour guide.' He rinsed his hands, then pulled two cocktail glasses brimming with something red and blue and exotic from the fridge.

'That looks interesting.'

'I like to experiment. I call this one Fijian Sky.'

She took the proffered glass, then walked to the balcony, held the glass up against the vermilion-streaked sunset. 'Perfect.' Nic followed and she turned, clinked her glass to his. 'To a tour guide extraordinaire *and* magical cocktail maker.'

He nodded. 'To muses.'

'Mmm.' She let the potent alcoholic flavour work its way down her throat. 'Speaking of muses, are you going to show me your work?'

'I've not been very productive of late.'

'My fault. But I'm not going to apologise.' Since he didn't offer any further information, or offer to show her around, she prompted, 'You have an office somewhere, I assume?'

'Upstairs.'

When he didn't move, she leaned closer, dragged a finger down his chest to his belt and stared up at him. 'You've seen mine, it's only fair you show me yours.'

An answering smile touched his lips and his eyes turned molten. 'Fair enough.' He rubbed his lips over hers before leading the way through the spacious living area.

The sound of water was everywhere, from the fountain to the salt-water infinity pool to an indoor garden in one corner with miniature waterfall.

Charlotte admired the Fijian décor throughout, raked ceilings and mahogany louvred panels open to allow air circulation, casual furniture around locally inspired carved tables. 'This is a beautiful home. Did you have a hand in designing it?'

'I had an interior designer come in and renovate,' he said as they climbed the stairs. 'It was pretty run-down when I bought it.' He flicked a switch and the room was filled with a cool ethereal glow.

'Wow.' She stared at the vast yet cluttered work space. A jumble of cables and computer paraphernalia took up half the room. Fantasy posters of alien landscapes covered every available wall surface. Metallic statues of mystical unearthly creatures with gleaming eyes of amber and blood-red stared at her from an array of bookshelves. A living vine of some sort grew in a pot by the window and wound its way across the ceiling.

'Dom Silverman,' she murmured, studying the multitude of awards above his computer. 'Your pseudonym?'

She noticed he hesitated at her mention of Silverman. Without comment, he switched on a computer and several screens lit up to form an almost 3-D landscape, alive with creatures and humans.

She leaned closer, eyes narrowed. 'Who's that girl?'

Damn. Nic had no idea how she'd persuaded him to

show her his office, his work, so easily. His alter ego, Dom Silverman. Yes, he did—with one finger and a hot look, it seemed she could make him forget everything, including caution. 'That's Reena.'

Charlotte peered closer. 'She looks like me...'

'Now that you mention it, she does. How about that?' He clicked a button and Reena wrapped herself in a silvery cloak and promptly disappeared.

'Well, bye bye, Reena,' Charlotte murmured and sipped from her glass, still watching the screens. 'So what's happening in Reena's world at the moment?'

'Nothing much lately. I've been playing around with some ideas for turning the games into a book when I've finished.' He gestured to the laptop he'd been working on for the past several evenings after seeing Charlotte to her bure. 'I've been working on computer games for eighteen years. I'm thinking maybe it's time for a change.'

'With your game's success, a publisher's bound to snap it up.'

'I'm not sure I want to publish it. Maybe it's more of a hobby. Like your underwear.'

'*Lingerie.*' She smiled. 'How did you get involved in computers?'

'When I was thirteen, the school ran a contest to design the school's website. I don't want to sound as if I'm blowing my own trumpet, but a teacher saw my potential and arranged for me to work in an office off the staff room outside of lesson times.'

'Darling, you can blow your trumpet any time you like.' She did that erotic thing with her finger again, except this time she didn't stop at his belt.

Eyes fused with hers, he gripped her hand and pressed it against his burgeoning erection. 'The prize was a computer.'

'And naturally you won.'

'Naturally.' He set his glass on the desk so he could run his other hand along the tops of her full breasts. 'I love when you wear this sarong…'

'I know.' Her voice was a husky purr, tempting him to unwind it and— 'But…I think I smell our dinner burning.'

'Damn.' It wasn't the only thing burning.

She stepped back, laughter mingling with the heat in her eyes. 'I'm so looking forward to it.'

He was too, and it wasn't dinner he was thinking about. But then, she already knew that.

CHAPTER TEN

THEY ate on the balcony with tea lights flickering in red glasses and fluorescent purple fairy lights strung along the balcony. The flames from the kerosene torches on the beach soared in the distance, the songs from the evening's *Meke* drifted on the air.

The fish was delicious, the wine chilled and fruity, the company perfect. Charlotte stirred sugar into her after-dinner coffee. The tropics would soon be a world away and, as much as she loved it here, her home was amongst the vineyards and close trusted friends. She craved the familiar and comfortable. Nic didn't fit into her cosy picture.

With his islander shirt and golden tan and idyllic lifestyle, Nic belonged in this place he'd made his home. Who could fail to be lured by the South Pacific's magic?

'You love it here, don't you?' she said, picking up her cup.

He leaned back on his chair, arms behind his head, an ankle resting on one bronzed thigh. 'I love the freedom and lifestyle. I can leave the windows open, come and go as I please. Sleep when I want or work all night. No one bothers me here.'

She noticed something dark flicker in the depths of his eyes at his mention of the last. 'You enjoy your solitude?'

'Sure I do.' His lips were set in a smile but his facial muscles tensed in a subtly different way.

She sipped slowly, watching him over her cup. When he was around people he was charming and attentive, romance was his forte. But when it came to anything deeper there was a barrier he wasn't ready or willing to lower.

She wanted to know why. She needed to know that there wasn't something inherently wrong with *her* that men didn't want to get involved. Or was she being overly sensitive? Because Nic couldn't have been more explicit about where they stood relationship-wise on their first night together here.

'You don't want a special someone to share your life?'

Any pretence at a smile he'd had, faded. 'I thought I made that clear.' He pushed off his chair and walked to the railing where the evening breeze fluttered his hair and a bamboo wind chime.

She remained seated but followed him with her gaze. Given a choice, how could anyone not want the comfort of loved ones around them? Seeing his solitude had made it so clear to her how much she missed her family. How much she wanted that feeling of connection and closeness again in the future. 'Ever?' she asked.

'We've been through all that.'

She heard the warning tone but she couldn't let it go. 'That's just sad.' She saw the tension stiffen his shoulders and said softly, 'Was your family life so b—?'

'That's enough.' He swung to face her. His eyes were dark, impenetrable.

'No. You know about mine. Why are you so defensive? Why do—?'

'It was only Mum and me, okay? When she bothered to come home.' He looked stunned, as if he hadn't intended to spill that information.

'Oh…' She trailed off, unable to imagine such a scenario and unsure how to respond. 'Working…?'

His mouth was a flat line, his jaw tight as a fist. 'Yeah, she worked, she worked damn hard. Then spent it playing poker and who knows what else, forgetting she had a son waiting at home for her.'

Charlotte wanted to hug the little boy he'd been, to comfort the man he was now, but she knew those were the last things he'd want from her, so she remained where she was. 'That must have been difficult.'

Nic shrugged. Then sighed. Charlotte was right. He'd fought to keep his past where it belonged but those defences were crumbling, the memories flashing back as if it were yesterday. He wanted to bury his face in her neck until it passed.

With Charlotte he found himself sharing things he'd never told anyone. 'I learned to cope. Even when she was alive, I was travelling solo. I guess at the very least you could say she taught me independence.'

'Were you living at home when she died?' Her tone was tentative.

'Technically, yes, but it was more the other way around— *she* was living with *me*. I hit the big time with my computer games when I was still in my teens. Money was no longer the problem.'

Charlotte's eyes filled with sadness, clouds on a soft rainy morning. 'Oh, the poor thing. Was she ill for a long time?'

He stared at her a beat before he realised she didn't get him at all. 'Save your sympathies—she wasn't sick a day in her life. She came out of the pub one day and stepped in front of a bus. Too busy counting her winnings—or more likely her losses—to pay attention to road rules.'

She blinked, obviously shocked. 'Oh. I'm sorry.'

'It's okay. I can't honestly say I missed her because I never saw her. From as far back as I remember, her life's routine never changed. Gone first thing in the morning, back at midnight.'

'Even when you were a kid?'

His mother was one thing but the dark days of his childhood were *not* up for discussion. He looked away, focused on the empty blackness of the sea and found it entirely appropriate. 'As I said, it taught me to rely on myself, by myself.'

He turned back to see her eyes still soft and sad, and, clenching his fists at his sides, he fought the mad impulse to reach out to her. Mad because she was trying to replace that loss with herself. She was a family girl looking for a family; something he couldn't give her. 'I don't know how to be any other way, babe.'

'Maybe that's because you've never tried.' She stood up and walked over to him, laid a hand on his arm. 'Maybe that's why you created the fantasy world,' she murmured. 'To compensate for what's lacking in your life.'

His lungs constricted at her perceptive insight into his innermost self. 'My life's just fine, thanks.'

She leaned back against the railing so that she could look him dead in the eye. 'What happened with…Angelica, was it?'

'How the hell…?'

She flicked a hand. 'Tenika might have mentioned her name. And the word "bad". In the same sentence.'

'God, a man can't leave two women together for less than a minute—'

'Nic. She cares about you. And you may not want to hear this, but I'm going to say it anyway so you'll just have to deal with it. So do I.'

Her eyes were wide and clear, her voice strong and determined yet at the same time filled with an offer of comfort, or at the very least a willingness to listen, whether he wanted to accept it or not. And he realised she'd risked his displeasure or worse. *Because she cared.* Something warm and unfamiliar slid through him. She deserved something of him in return.

'Remember that first morning here I accused you of spying in my garden?' He looked away, out to sea. 'You can blame Angelica for my paranoia.' Even the name still sent a shudder down his spine. 'The woman had beauty and brains. Enough intelligence to steal my work and enough audacity to pass it off as hers.'

'Oh, Nic, that's appalling.'

'Make no mistake, I got it back through the courts.'

'How did you meet?'

'At a conference in the States. She was a computer programmer from Sydney.'

'You were lovers?'

He glared at her. 'What do you think?'

'I wondered only because I can't imagine anyone doing that to someone they cared about.'

'That's just it, she never did—care, that is. It was all about the games, and how she could use me. That's when I decided to take another name and write my Utopian trilogy. Nic Russo no longer exists in online gaming.' Pulling out his mobile, he rang through to Reception.

'What are you doing?'

'Arranging for your luggage to be brought up and checking you out.'

'But—'

'You're staying here with me tonight.'

Moments later, in his bedroom, his fingers rushed to peel the sarong from her body as he'd been itching to do all evening. But as he looked into her eyes, the need for speed was replaced by a new demand that was no less urgent. The need not only to claim, but to possess.

Passion rose as haste slowed. Time to absorb the drift of silky skin against his palms, the warmth of her breath mingling with his own, her lush curves that melted against him like sun-warmed honey. *Just a woman*, but the sensations shivered through him like quicksilver over smooth onyx.

Charmed.

The glow from the fairy lights outside his window bathed her in the mysteriously alluring shades of indigo and magenta, making him willing to forget why he'd never had a woman in this room since Angelica.

Her eyes were clear as still water, reaching inside him and touching the secret places in his heart that no woman had ever come close to. Understanding, accepting.

'Charlotte...' His murmur was low and heartfelt as he skimmed his hands over the slope of her breast, the flare of her hips. It wasn't for ever, but for tonight—one last night—he would take everything she offered.

Charlotte didn't want Nic to take her to the airport. Saying goodbye to this magical island was hard enough, saying goodbye to Nic, effectively ending their time together, all but impossible.

So she slid out of his bed before dawn, dressed quickly in the dimness, then rang for a taxi downstairs and slipped back to the resort's reception area a two-minute walk away. She'd send him an email or text to let him know she'd arrived home safely. And that would be the end of it.

A few hours later, in the airline's business lounge at Tullamarine, ten minutes before her flight to Adelaide was due to board, she tapped in Suzette's number on her mobile. 'Hi, Suz, I'm back. Or in Melbourne at least.'

'Well, it's about time.' Charlotte heard the smile in her best friend's voice. 'You did tell me not to call so I didn't.'

'And I appreciate it.'

'I know you needed the time to think about everything, but I thought about *you* while I froze through two of the coldest weeks this winter. Those golden beaches and hot tropical nights. Please tell me you had a wild romantic fling with some gorgeous guy and you've forgotten all about that creep who didn't deserve you.'

Charlotte knew Suzette wasn't entirely serious because the Charlotte Suzette knew would never have done such a thing. 'Uh-huh.'

There was a stunned pause. 'What? *What?* Fill me in *now*,' she demanded. 'What's his name and what does he do?'

'Nic Russo.' Just saying his name made her heart skip a beat. 'He writes computer games; the interactive, out-of-this-world kind. If you look up *Utopian Twilight* you'll see what I mean—amazing. *He's* amazing and—' She realised she was talking too fast, gushing in fact, and pressed those wayward lips together.

'*And...?* Where's he from? Are you seeing him again?'

'He...' *Reality check, Charlotte. He doesn't want what I want. There's nothing for us*. A band tightened around her chest and her eyes blurred suspiciously. 'No, I'm not seeing him again. It was a fling, Suz. That wild romantic fling thing.'

'Yeah, but...'

'It's over. Finished. Isn't that what you told me to do? Forget *the creep* and enjoy myself and come back a different woman? I took your advice.' And would live with the consequences. 'I'll be home by tonight if you want to come round. I've got an idea for a fashion show to raise funds for a Fijian school I visited.' *And I could sure use the company.* But she didn't say it because it would make losing Nic more real when he'd never been hers to lose.

'Love to, Charlie, but I'm still in the Riverland at the bridal fashion seminar. I'll be back soon. I'll let you know as soon as. In the meantime, email me some details on the show. I'd love to be involved.'

'Okay.' Charlotte caught the downbeat tone in her own voice and forced a smile, suddenly desperate to end this call before she spilled her guts. 'Catch up with you then.'

As Charlotte disconnected a young woman in a business skirt and white blouse rose from a nearby seat and approached with a smile. Charlotte recognised her instantly from Adelaide's social events. Great, the press; just what she didn't need.

'Ms Dumont, welcome back. I was sorry to hear about your recent split with Mr Edwards. What—?'

'Our lives took different directions.' Charlotte concentrated on sliding her phone into her bag. 'Changed priorities. That's all I have to say on the matter.'

'How did you enjoy Fiji?'

'It was great, thanks.'

Bright blue eyes gleamed with speculation. 'What are your plans now?'

'I really don't have… Wait…' Maybe she could use the press to her advantage for a change. 'I intend hosting a charity event soon, to raise money for a Fijian school. I'll be making an announcement to the Adelaide press soon.'

'Any particular reason for your ch—?'

'That's all for now.' Gathering her luggage together, she began walking. 'I have a flight to catch.'

Nic frowned at his black computer screen while he fiddled with a miniature paper dragonfly on his desk. Charlotte had left without a word. Walked out of his life without a

backward glance. Hadn't even left a note—just the imprint
of her head on the pillow and her lingering fragrance. He
sent the dragonfly soaring across the room.

So what was wrong with that scene? Why did his morning seem heavy with cloud when the sun was shining
cheerfully on the palms outside his window? After all,
wasn't he habitually guilty of the same casual morning-
after behaviour?

*It was wrong because he'd not been the one with the
final say.*

So he told himself he'd taken a long-overdue break. He'd
enjoyed the company of a beautiful woman, now it was
time to get back to work. He clicked keys, waited impa-
tiently for his world to load. The screen lit up, the familiar scene appeared and he was home. In control. Supreme
Commander of his Universe.

Scene: maroon sky, blood-red moon, splinters of ob-
sidian thrusting skyward. Onyx One, chained to the sheer
cliff. Screaming wind blowing up from the volcano's fiery
furnace below. Reena to the rescue on a winged amethyst
creature, hair flying behind her, golden sword held high
in one hand...

Charlotte.

Swearing, he shoved at the desk, his chair rolling back
over the parquetry floor. He ploughed his hands through
his hair and ordered himself to cool it. But all he could see
was Charlotte in his bed, her beautiful body spread across
his sheets like liquid gold, her gaze intense, her hands all
over him wielding her signature brand of charm.

And last night he'd let his mouth run away with his
common sense and told her things about himself he'd never
told anyone.

Work, he reminded himself, pushing all erotic thoughts

and bad judgements and trust issues away. He had a program to write and by God he was going to do it.

His determination paid off and he worked solidly for the rest of the day and well into the night, only rolling into bed for a couple of hours' sleep before doing it all again.

Late in the afternoon on the following day, he rewarded himself with a swim, then sat in the shady surrounds to catch up with the real world in the day's local newspaper.

But on page three, his own face stared back at him, beside a large graphic that could have been plucked from one of his games. The caption read, *Dom Silverman: The Secret World of Nic Russo?* Included in the article was a small photo of him and Charlotte on board a yacht and speculation about their relationship.

He didn't bother to read it. Betrayal stabbed at him, its black stain spreading like sin in front of his eyes as he wrenched upright and snatched up his mobile.

When her phone rang and Charlotte saw Nic's number, her heart stopped, then began pounding. How many times in the last twenty-four hours had she started to ring him before reminding herself Nic didn't want anything more meaningful than what they'd had?

Then remembering how she'd left him without a word, she pressed the connect button with a mix of excitement and apprehension. 'Hello, Nic. Did you get my text—?'

'Why, Charlotte?' The words weren't what she'd expected, nor were they spoken in that sexy tone she'd grown so accustomed to hearing; they were tight and remote and filled with such cold anger a chill shivered down her spine.

'I'm sorry.' Her hands started to tremble; she pressed her free hand against her heart. 'I thought it was the best way, under the cir—'

'Was it for the money? Your inheritance not what you expected?' His sarcastic tone tore at her sudden fragility.

'What are you talking about?'

'That reporter on the beach,' he said in frigid tones that burned and froze at the same time. 'You told him about me. About Dom Silverman.'

'No! That's not true.' Her legs turned to water and she sank to the floor. 'What happened?'

'An article in the newspaper *happened*. Interesting co-incidence, wouldn't you say, that it appears the day after you skip off back to Australia?'

He made it sound as if she'd done a moonlight flit with his life savings. 'Oh, Nic, no…' Charlotte's fingers clutched her phone tighter, pressing it to her ear as if willing the words to convince him. 'Please, Nic. Believe me. I'd *never* do that to you.' She closed her eyes. 'I swear on my parents' graves that it wasn't me.'

A long, tense silence followed. Surely he knew her well enough to understand that she'd never use the memory of her parents in such a way if she didn't mean it?

'How the hell, then, did they find out?' He spoke each word as if chewing on leather.

'I don't know. Oh…' Unless that reporter at Tullamarine… Could she have been listening in on her conversation with Suzette? Charlotte tried to recall what she'd said, then wished the floor would open up and swallow her. 'Oh, no…'

'Okay, let's have it.'

She tried to explain, tripping over her words. She'd referred to Nic by his real name…but she'd mentioned *Utopian Twilight* in the same breath. A couple of mouse clicks and anyone would have the knowledge at their fingertips.

'You still don't know how to deal with the paparazzi, do you?' She could practically hear his teeth grinding together. 'Never, *never*, say or do anything in public that you don't want the world to know about.'

'Nic…' She willed herself not to cry. 'I don't know what to—'

'Tell me your address and I'll send a car for you tomorrow at five p.m. He'll make sure you're not followed and you'll meet me at Montefiore Hill at six.'

North Adelaide's Montefiore Hill overlooking the city was a favourite spot for snogging and lovers' trysts.

Not this time.

She heard the abrupt click as he disconnected. He was flying back to Adelaide tomorrow. Not for a close reunion but a confrontation.

CHAPTER ELEVEN

WHEN the car ferrying Charlotte cruised into Montefiore Hill's car park during a rain storm, she knew the red sports car parked alongside had to be Nic's. She got a quick glimpse of him as he exited with an umbrella and opened the passenger door for her.

He didn't waste time with rain-drenched greetings, bundling her inside and rounding the car while the rain drummed on the roof. The cab drove off and he slid in beside her, smelling of winter and wet wool.

Black jumper, black jeans, black eyes. A formidable contrast to her vibrant island lover and her heart thundered with apprehension—and desire. Even under such circumstances her body seemed to have a will of its own.

'Nic...' she began, then trailed off beneath his gaze. To escape its intensity she looked at the city lights through the blurred windscreen.

He shifted closer, his warmth invading her space, but he didn't touch her. 'I'm not happy with you, Charlotte.'

'I screwed up big time, didn't I?' When he didn't reply, she went on, 'I hope you trust me enough to know I'd never do anything to hurt you. I understand you don't trust easily after everything you've told me, but I—'

'I've decided you were telling the truth.'

She let out a slow breath. 'You don't know what a relief

it is to hear you say that.' Even if his words were clipped and remote. She allowed herself to relax against the soft leather seat for the first time in what felt like a life sentence.

'So now we deal with it. Together.'

She turned to him, incredulous. Droplets of water still shimmered in his hair. 'I'd've thought you wouldn't want anything more to do with me.'

'I've given it plenty of thought over the past twenty-four hours. We all make mistakes.'

'That's very generous of you but I don't deserve it. Because of me, you've lost your writing anonymity—'

'It's not the worst thing that's ever happened to me.' Watching her, he stroked the ends of her hair with light fingers. 'Maybe it was the universe's way of telling me it was time.'

'And now our names will be linked and splashed all over the gossip columns and—'

'The name Nic Russo is known in Fiji but it doesn't have the same media exposure in Australia.'

'Until now.'

He acknowledged that but smoothed the hair behind her ear and drifted his fingers to her cheek. 'I'm more concerned about the Barossa wine princess; I know how you hate publicity.'

'I can handle it. I'm getting better at it.' Her breathing stalled at the barely there caress and she leaned into his touch, drew in his familiar scent. 'You didn't have to come all the way to Adelaide to hold my hand.'

'True. But maybe it's not only your hand I want to hold.' His voice dropped to its husky low register as he reached over her and the back of her seat reclined smoothly. He fused his mouth to hers, swallowing any reply she might have made, and his taste—warmer and smoother than the best whisky and all the sweeter for its familiarity. One hand slid beneath her jumper and up beneath the edge of her bra to cup her breast and tease a nipple.

'Nic…wait…' she managed when he finally lifted his lips to tug on her ear lobe. 'We're in a public place.'

'Relax. No one's around.' He leaned back slightly to look at her, those sensual lips curved, his eyes twinkling with the city's reflected light. 'You've never been parking in a Ferrari before?'

'Um…no.'

He unsnapped the top stud on her jeans, slid his hand down her belly and inside her panties. 'About time you did, then…'

Urgency pummelled Nic as she arched against him, her moans echoing his. He plunged his fingers into her wet heat while the rain continued to lash the roof. A few frantic seconds and he had her jeans down to her knees, his own jeans unzipped and—at last—he was ruthlessly riding her where only she could take him. No patience, no control, no finesse. Just blind, searing passion as they flew together over that mindless pinnacle.

They readjusted their clothes in silence. Nic had been fooling himself into thinking this thing with Charlotte was finished. He wanted more—just a few days, a couple of weeks maybe, get her out of his system, then he could focus on work. 'Come back to my apartment.'

She was finger-combing her hair but paused to look at him, her eyes wide, her lips plump. Ravished. Adorable. 'I'll drive you home tomorrow,' he told her, then leaned across to smooth those lips with his and murmured, 'I want to make love with you again. All night.'

'Me too,' she murmured back.

Moments later Nic swung out of the deserted park and headed for Glenelg. Probably faster than he should, considering the slippery road conditions but he couldn't wait to get her fully naked, to feel her body pressed up against his again.

'I guess you'll be going straight back to Fiji, then,' she said as they cruised through an amber light. 'Especially with this cold weather.'

'I'm here now; might as well stay on a bit.' He glanced her way. Her hair was temptingly tousled, her hands clasped tight on her lap. 'Are you still planning to go ahead with the fashion show idea? I could stick around if it's not too far away, give you some support. If you'd like.'

'Yes, I am, and I'd love for you to be here for it. Suzette's supplying the bridal gowns and formal wear and the models and I'm going to contact the attendees with money to burn. Shouldn't take more than a couple of weeks to organise.'

'Bridal?'

'Suzette's speciality.'

'No *lingerie*?' When she didn't answer, he flicked her a grin. 'Brides want something special at the end of the big day to wow their grooms with, don't they? You make a stunning model—I've seen you firsthand, remember.'

'I know what you're thinking, Nic, and you can forget it.'

'Pity.'

'Since you're here,' she went on, switching topics fast, 'those opera tickets I mentioned are for tomorrow night, if you'd like to join me. If you're not busy…'

'Guess I could give it a try.' He squeezed her thigh. 'On the condition that you come home with me after.'

'Deal.'

The following morning, Charlotte slid out of bed before Nic woke. In their hurry to get naked last night, she hadn't given the apartment more than a glance, but she took note of the bathroom now as she coiled her hair on top of her head and waited for the water temperature to rise.

Black. Masculine. No pretty-smelling soaps—and why would there be?—just a shelf stocked haphazardly with the usual generic bottles and shaving gear. Glass and chrome gleamed in the sunlight slanting through the frosted window, the lack of colour relieved by a couple of thick red towels. It was spacious enough with a deep spa and a shower stall big enough for two.

Ignoring the supermarket-brand gel dangling from one of the twin heads, she lathered up with her own tiny 'Charlotte's Meadow' travel soap, glad she'd had it in her handbag.

The cheery voice of a radio announcer was her first and only clue that she was no longer alone. She glanced up and noticed twin speakers mounted on the wall, catching a shadowy blur of movement beyond the steamy glass screen as she did so.

'Mind if I join you?'

Just hearing that husky morning voice turned her knees to jelly as the screen door opened and Nic stepped in behind her.

'I…ah…' She bit back a moan as his hands slid over her shoulders to tweak her nipples into tight little buds. 'I thought…you were asleep.'

'I was.' He nipped at the side of her neck with his lips. 'But then I smelled this perfume and had to investigate.' He leaned further, took the soap from her hands. 'It's been driving me mad for the past two weeks.'

'You can thank my emergency soap supply, then.'

'Of course,' he murmured. 'On every princess's travel essentials list.' His big body was pressed up behind her and he was obviously ready to get on with things.

'Laugh if you like,' she said, primly. 'I'm not going to change.'

'And I wouldn't want you to. It was made for you, this scent,' he murmured, nipping her ear lobe, his breath mingling with the steam that rose around them, closing them in, shutting everything else out.

'As a matter of fact, it was.' It was hard to concentrate when his erection was nudging her backside and his hands were busy drawing soapy circles around her breasts. 'Exclusively… In Paris… Years ago.' It had cost a bomb but she still imported it on a regular basis.

'So what can I smell… Jasmine?'

'And honeysuckle, sweet mandarin, black rose… amongst other things…'

'It reminds me of a lake at sunset with mist swirling low on the ground and the sky burnished with colour.'

'You should be a writer…'

'And you're there, facing the water, in something long and smooth and glowing like fire to match the sky. Then I come up behind you and kiss your neck like this…' His lips nipped and pressed across her nape. 'And the dress dissolves like gold dust under my hands.' Those hands glided over her skin, and every dip, every curve he touched sang his praises.

'Your perfume was the first thing I noticed about you,' he murmured against her ear.

'It was?'

'You were in front of me in the check-in queue at Tullamarine.'

'Oh…' How could she not have known? How could she not have felt this connection between them that had become as much a part of her as the air she breathed?

An arm reached in front of her and he set the soap on its dish, nudging closer. She spread her legs in invitation, or maybe it was surrender, as he pushed inside her, holding her upright with his strength and warmth.

'And I fantasised about doing this…' he said, pushing deeper, harder, his hands sliding over her belly, and lower, between her thighs where she wanted him with the most desperate of wants.

And Nic couldn't imagine a better way to start the day than with a fantasy come to life. 'I have to tell you, the back of your neck's an obsession of mine.'

He played light fingertips over her nape, worked slowly up from the base of her skull and into her silky hair. And she responded like a harp carved and tuned exclusively for him, her sweet sighs like angels' music to his ears. Working his fingers higher over her scalp, he felt the shiver that moved through her.

'That feels…amazing.'

'So do you…' He thrust once more—deeply—and her slick heat tightened like a glove around him. 'So do you.'

They ate breakfast overlooking the ocean. The rain had passed but it was still cold outside, the wind hurling itself against the glass and whipping up white tops. Charlotte studied his apartment, minimalist in the extreme, compared to his Fijian house, which felt like a home. Miles of glass, stern black and chrome furniture—not even a cushion or house plant to soften the austerity. A typical bachelor pad.

Munching on a slice of toast, she wondered if he brought women here, but was beginning to realise his privacy was paramount. No doubt he graced the bed of many a woman's boudoir, however. 'You have an office here too?'

He indicated a closed door on the far side of the living room. 'It's pretty basic but the light and the view make up for it.'

'Loads of inspiration, then.'

He poured himself another cup of coffee. 'I do my most creative work in Fiji. Adelaide's mainly where I work on the programs.'

Charlotte rose, carried her dishes to the dishwasher, loaded them. 'Since I'm at Glenelg, I might take a stroll down Jetty Road before I leave, if you're not in a hurry.'

'Fine by me.' He rose too. 'I'm going for a run on the beach.' He stretched, giving her a glimpse of tanned taut abdomen beneath the hem of his windcheater. 'If I know women at all, I'll be back before you but just in case…' He walked to the fridge, took a key off a hook, handed it to her.

Not wanting to disturb him if he was working, Charlotte let herself in an hour later. When she didn't see Nic, she called softly and knocked at his office door, turned the knob.

Locked.

Her buoyant mood slipped a bit. More interested in spending time with Nic than browsing boutiques, she'd cut her trip to the popular shopping strip short, and beaten him back. The locked door in his own home was also a surprise. Was that his habit or was it to keep her out? Did he still not trust her? No, it was an added security measure, she told herself. His work was valuable, and after what Angelica had done who could blame him?

On the positive side, having the place to herself gave her time to arrange her purchase of four plump red cushions along the sofa before he returned. She set the happy plant on the glass coffee table. A nice welcome home, she decided, pleased with the effect, and the cushions would be a reminder of their time together every time he sat on the sofa to admire the view.

She spent the time tidying his bedroom and en suite, then progressed to the kitchen. She was wiping down the benches when he blew in looking wild and windswept and bringing with him the scent of the sea.

She used the tea towel to wipe her hands. 'Hi.'

'Back already?' His expression told her he wasn't used to coming home to company. 'What woman cuts short a shopping expedition?'

'This woman.' She reached up on tiptoe to kiss him. 'I was beginning to think you'd run back to Fiji.'

He tucked his hands in the back pockets of her jeans to pull her hips closer but his eyes held a hint of reproach. 'Not without telling you, I wouldn't.'

'Okay, message received and understood.'

Nic kissed her again, still somewhat distracted by the newness and surprise of having someone waiting for him in his apartment. 'I didn't expect you back yet so I stopped in at that café down the beach a bit...' He trailed off at the sight of his cushion-festooned sofa, the greenery on the table, and heard the first alarm bell clang. 'What's all this?'

'I thought they'd make it a bit more homely.'

'I don't need cushions.' Or homely. Cushions were women's work; they did *not* suit a bachelor's apartment. 'I hardly ever sit here.'

'Well, you should,' she said, behind him. 'You shouldn't be chained to your desk all day...'

'It's what I do. And I won't be here long enough to fuss over any plant.'

'Oh... I didn't think of that. Jeez, I'm an idiot.'

He heard the confusion and embarrassment and felt like a jerk, but it didn't change the fact that she'd altered their relationship. Did she think he was staying on indefinitely? Did she think she could persuade him with little gifts of domesticity? How many women had plied him with similar gestures? A pot of home-made soup, a towel embroidered with his name, hoping to lure him to the altar and set up a joint bank account.

'It's not that I don't appreciate the thought,' he said, 'but—'

'Don't worry about it—give them to charity. It's fine.'

Nic knew from experience when a woman said 'fine' in that tone, it meant anything but. 'I'm going to take a quick shower, then I'll drive you home.' Maybe he could smooth things over on the way.

'No need, I've booked a cab.' She spoke crisply, her expression devoid of emotion, and glanced at her watch. 'He'll be here any minute now. I'll go downstairs and get out of your way.'

'Charlotte…' *Wait.* An odd panic worked its way through the annoyance. 'I said I'd drive you, just give me a damn m—'

'The opera ticket.' She dug into her bag, pulled it out and slapped it on the kitchen bench, eyes sparking now. 'This way you can suit yourself whether you come or not.'

Charlotte waited in the foyer for Nic to show, pacing the thick carpet, ignoring the subtle glances of recognition cast her way. She'd not been out in public since the break-up and knew there'd be gossip in tomorrow's paper. It would have been so satisfying to have had a partner to flaunt tonight and not to have to climb into a cab sad and alone at the end of the evening. Not that she wanted to *flaunt* Nic, especially since she'd revealed his identity to the press.

I just want to be with him.

Biting back a sigh, she checked the time. Did she really expect him to show after this morning's debacle? She'd done what he'd made clear he didn't want from her; she'd gone domestic on him.

The last bell rang. Most patrons had already disappeared into the auditorium. She should go home. There was no way she could enjoy the performance under the circumstances.

As she turned to leave she saw Nic approaching and her heart wanted to weep and dance at the same time. This gorgeous sexy man in a snappy dark suit and tie was here to meet her. She had to force herself to walk sedately across the carpet and not to fling her arms around his neck.

'Traffic was heavier than I expected,' he said, smelling freshly showered as he tucked her arm through his and walked towards the auditorium doors, which were already closing.

'You're here now.' That was all that mattered.

'Charlotte.' He stopped, looked down at her, eyes troubled. 'I shouldn't have reacted that way this morning.' He shook his head. 'Everything about you, everything with you… It's different.'

'I know.' And it scared her too.

'So what's the verdict on opera?' Charlotte watched the street lights flicker over Nic's face as he drove them back to his apartment.

'I was too busy watching you.'

Always the smooth talker, was Nic, and she basked for a moment in the glow. But only for a moment because this morning's exchange was still recent and raw. 'Seriously though, did you enjoy it?'

'I think I'm with your father on this.'

'Okay… In that case, thanks for coming with me and giving it a try. You can chalk it up to a new experience.'

'It was an experience watching you in your familiar environment.'

'Yeah. Lady Mitchell's probably on her phone right now, spreading the word.'

'Does that bother you?'

'No.' Knowing that Mum's circle of friends would gossip and speculate as a result of bumping into Grace Mitchell no longer mattered.

They parked beneath Nic's building, then took the stairs to the ground floor and walked the long way round to the entrance so they could see the ocean roll in.

'This has been a *wonderful* evening,' she said, hugging her upper arms against the chill blowing off the sea.

The wind combed Charlotte's hair so that it streamed behind her like ribbons and Nic couldn't resist running his hand through the silky strands. 'It's not over yet.'

'Nic…' She turned, her eyes as silvery soft as sea mist with a fragility that tugged at something deep within him. 'This…thing…'

'It's okay,' he told her softly, and realised he meant it. 'Different is okay.'

She smiled slowly and it was like watching the sun coming out at midnight as she took his hands in hers and led him towards the lift. 'Yes. It is.'

Wholly absorbed—*charmed*—with the vision in front of him, Nic followed. The doors slid closed, shutting off the sounds of the sea and enclosing them in stainless-steel walls as it began to rise.

Dragging off her scarf, she wound it behind his head and pulled him close. The lift jolted and the lights dimmed for a second or two before the lift resumed its ascent. 'Uh-oh,' she murmured against his chin. 'Ever been stuck in a lift?'

Nic's pulse skipped a beat and adrenaline spiked through his system. 'No.' He didn't tell her he always took the stairs.

'So do you want to be?'

'Be what…?' He was finding it hard to concentrate on

her words when his vision was turning dark and his pulse was drumming and he *couldn't breathe*.

She flicked the buttons of her coat undone. 'Stuck in a lift...'

'Not particularly.' A bead of sweat trickled down his back.

Tugging on the ends of her scarf, she pressed her body hard up against his. 'Are you sure? Lifts have a stop button somewhere, don't they? I imagine it could be—'

'Don't even think about it.' Did his voice sound too harsh, too loud? *Stop!* he yelled silently, using his self-help technique. Forcing his breathing to slow, he watched the number for his floor wink on and let out a private sigh.

'Too late, you've just lost your chance.' She danced out ahead of him, her heels tapping on the polished boards, her scarf trailing behind her. It gave him a moment to suck in air.

Shrugging off her coat, she tossed it over the sofa then turned, eyes bright and playful. She slid the strap of her black dress off one shoulder and flicked him a sultry look beneath her lashes. 'Want to see what I'm wearing underneath?'

'Later.' Self-disgust was a dark and lonely place. 'I've got some urgent matters to attend to. I'll be in my office.' He kissed her bare shoulder to take the sting out of what she'd see as a rejection, but he wasn't up for sharing his shortcomings. 'You warm up the bed for me, I'll be along in a few moments.'

Charlotte awoke in the darkness, disoriented, and aware that something had disturbed her sleep. Some sound of distress? Turning her head on the pillow, she saw the empty space beside her. She vaguely recalled Nic coming to bed at some stage. But now the sheets were twisted and thrown back. It was four-twenty a.m.

She slipped out of bed, pulled on his shirt from the bottom of the bed, then made her way carefully along the unfamiliar hallway till she reached the living room. She saw Nic on the balcony facing the sea, *naked*, his overlong hair blown back by the wind. Solitary. Lost. Alone.

I love him.

The knowledge—its dazzle and the dismay—ripped through her, body and soul, and she stumbled backwards. No. Not now, not with him: a man who'd made it quite clear he was happy with their temporary relationship. A man who'd told her he didn't know how to be anyone but that lonely figure standing on the balcony.

Because her legs were trembling, she sank onto the nearest available chair. *Count to five. Breathe. This is not allowed to happen—he's a friend, a lover. That's all.*

She wasn't aware how long she sat in the dark, watching him, listening to the hum of the fridge, the sound of her heart drumming in her ears and convincing herself it was hero worship. He'd rescued her, right? When he went back to Fiji it would fade. She just needed time and distance.

He must be freezing his butt off out there.

Her heart shivered in empathy, and she hesitated, torn between offering support in whatever way might be appropriate and afraid he'd not welcome it.

Maybe he liked to plot when inspiration struck. Maybe he worked best at night and naked. She was hardly familiar with his sleeping habits.

He turned so that his face was in profile. From a few feet away on the other side of the glass, she could see the lowered ridge of brow, the tight flat line of his mouth, his hands fisted on the glass balcony. He didn't look contemplative, he looked disturbed, yet he'd been fine until they'd got to his apartment.

She thought of going back to bed but she simply could not walk away and leave him to the cold winter's night. She picked up her coat that she'd left on the sofa earlier.

He turned, surprise crossing his gaze when she opened the glass door.

'Nic…?'

A guarded wariness smothered the surprise, then a hint of that playboy grin flirted with the corner of his mouth. It didn't reach his eyes. 'Hey, babe, that shirt looks better on you than it does on me.'

'Nic, it's freezing out here.'

He shook his head. 'Go back to bed, Charlotte.'

'You'll catch a chill.' She held out her coat.

'Don't give me that mummy routine.' But he took it, shrugged it on. 'Happy now?'

'Not really. And sorry about the "routine"; that's the way I am. Would you like something warm to drink?' She bit her lip. *Stop. Now.*

'I'm right, thanks.' He lifted the brandy bottle from the table beside him, splashed liquid into a tumbler with a clink of glass on glass.

'Bad dreams?' she ventured. 'I thought I heard…' She shook her head once—a man like Nic would die before he'd admit it.

'I'm working.' He took a healthy gulp of his brandy, then studied the bottom of his glass. 'Dreams give me a different perspective. Hero's got himself in a bit of a tight spot.'

'Are you sure that's—?'

'Inspiration strikes at the oddest times.' He didn't look at her. 'I do my best work at night.' His gaze lifted skywards. 'There's something about the stars at this time of the morning. They look closer somehow. You feel connected to something bigger than yourself.'

Maybe. But one thing was abundantly clear—he didn't want or need her company. She gritted her teeth against the chill and the hurt at being shut out and stepped away, both literally and figuratively. 'I'll leave you to your inspiration, then.'

CHAPTER TWELVE

FOR what was left of the night Nic found refuge in his office and distraction in his cyber world. Hours later, as dawn lightened the sky, he watched the surf roll in over an indigo sea. The never-ending horizon cut the sky, sharp and precise as a blade.

He breathed in slowly and deeply, until his lungs were full and his mind clear of the suffocating darkness that had plagued him since childhood.

His personal and private hell had obviously disturbed Charlotte's sleep too. Had he cried out? By God, he hoped not. Bad enough that he'd barely got out of the damn lift without making an ass of himself.

He'd hurt her. He'd seen it in her eyes when he'd not taken her to bed, craving her comfort even as he did so. *Because she cared*. She was falling for him and that hadn't been the plan.

And against all his rules, he'd fallen for her too. *Big mistake, Nic*. What woman would want a guy with his baggage and his secrets and his phobias? Charlotte Dumont was a long-term, commitment-driven, family kind of girl, and he didn't know how to do family. Nor did he need mothering, for pity's sake. He'd done okay without it his entire life.

And she was one of those women he avoided—the kind who liked to discuss *feelings*.

Not Nic. He hadn't discussed feelings since he'd told his mother he was scared because it had got dark while she'd been gone and he couldn't reach the light switch. Had talking about it changed anything? Not a whit. Had talking about it made the dark seem more real, more menacing, more stifling? You bet.

But in his Utopian world, he wasn't confined, he was free. He could be anyone he wanted, do what he wanted.

Not with Charlotte. So with what was left of their time together, he'd be that fun casual guy she'd met at the airport. Decision made, he got back to work.

She must have slept, because the next thing Charlotte knew, Nic was dressed and alert and suggesting breakfast in one of the little cafés downstairs.

As they ate she saw no trace of the man she'd left on the balcony, just the usual carefree, flirty Nic. *That* man she could deal with and keep her true feelings hidden.

'Red kitchen, red towels, red car,' she said as she settled into the passenger seat for the drive home.

'A Ferrari's gotta be red.' He glanced at her jeans and mushroom-coloured top. 'I'd like to see *you* in red. Fire-engine-red silk... Hoo, baby, you'd look hot.'

'Red's not a colour I wear. Unless it's lingerie.'

His eyes flicked to her breasts and he jiggled his eyebrows as he turned the ignition. 'So are you going to model any of that red *lingerie* for me some time soon?'

'Maybe.' Persuasive, he was. Seductive and irresistible.

As they cruised out of the underground garage and onto the main road, he said, 'Just because you don't wear red, doesn't mean you can't try a change now and then.'

Oh, but she *had* changed. Maybe he didn't realise he'd brought about change in her and in so many ways. Good changes. She'd left the woman Flynn had known, and rejected, behind. Nic had forced her to look at life in a different way and she was going to miss him terribly for that.

Not only that.

She rubbed a hand over the ache in her heart that was growing every day, every hour, every minute. She saw many things differently now. What she'd had with Flynn was a pale imitation of the real thing. Like comparing beige sack cloth with red silk.

The eighty-minute drive to the Barossa Valley gave her time to ring around for attendees for the fashion show and take her mind off Nic. Yesterday she'd locked in her first choice for a venue, available in two weeks due to a late cancellation.

She tapped in the first name on her list. 'Lady Alexandra? Good morning, it's Charlotte Dumont.'

Nic tuned out as Charlotte made her endless list of calls. *Lady Alexandra, Sir William Beaumont, Mrs Hartford-Jones.* This up-scale event with South Australia's landed gentry was going to be a new experience for him.

They were driving into the Barossa now, the road flanked with bare vines. Low hills the colour of porridge rolled along the horizon. They passed a winery, its cellar door doing a thriving business in the middle of the week with a couple of tourist buses parked outside.

Would Charlotte use her inheritance to set up something similar as she'd originally intended? She knew the wine industry and he could see her interacting with people. But her expertise in fashion design was marketable and more unique.

Eventually he followed her directions down a private road, which widened into a circular drive around a smooth emerald lawn big enough to play a round of golf on. Bright spring bulbs danced in the breeze at the base of a two-tier fountain directly in front of the massive front door.

The home itself was a rambling two-storey blue-stone. White pillars supported a wide wrap-around veranda on both floors.

'Come on,' she told him, excitement bubbling through her voice as she climbed out. 'It's my turn to show *you* around.'

He followed her up the shallow steps and waited while she decoded the security. Inside, the house was no less impressive. A Scarlett O'Hara staircase, stained glass, Persian rugs. It smelled of floor polish and a hell of a lot of old money.

He stared up at the foyer's enormous chandelier. 'How many rooms does this place have?'

'Twenty-two. That's including the cellar, which has its own chandelier,' she said, following his gaze.

'A chandelier in a cellar?'

'Not just a cellar, it's also a place for entertaining. I'll show you later.'

Not if he could help it. 'And you live here alone?' He looked down at her and the flush of excitement faded; sadness clouded her eyes.

'Suzette stays over sometimes. Since Flynn left.' She seemed to shrink in stature. 'I can't sell it,' she said quietly. 'It's all I have left of my family.' She turned away and started walking towards the back of the house. 'Go for a wander—I'll put on some coffee.'

He suspected her snappy departure didn't have as much to do with refreshments as the unwillingness to look him in the eye. And it shouldn't be that way, he thought, climbing the stairs. He should be offering support. Coming back to an empty home under such circumstances had to be tough.

But how could he when he didn't believe her decision to stay here and dwell on the past was in her best interest? He knew that to tell her selling up was a better option would not go down well.

He ambled down the wide hallway, past bedrooms and guest suites filled with antique furniture, then paused at the doorway to what was obviously her parents' bedroom.

'I've left it exactly as it was,' she said behind him. Her shoulder brushed his as she slipped into the room. She walked to the bay window, fingered a tapestry on one of two French-polished chairs facing each other over a round matching table. 'Mum's cross-stitch that she was working on.'

Nic saw a half-finished jigsaw spread out on the table and a pair of men's spectacles set neatly to the side.

'They used to sit here together in the evenings. They believed in having at least an hour every night to talk to each other without the distraction of TV.'

'Charlotte…' He walked towards her slowly, the back of his neck prickling as though the room's occupants were still there. And to Charlotte, they were. 'This isn't healthy, sweetheart. You need to move on.'

He lifted a hand and might have touched her cheek but she sidestepped out of reach, her posture stiff, arms crossed like a shield, lips a thinned white slash in a whiter face.

'And what the hell would you know about it, Nic?'

Yeah, Nic, what the hell? His hand fell to his side, curling into a fist as a tide of dark emotions ripped through him. This world—Charlotte's world—was an alien landscape to him. His teeth clicked together audibly and he stepped back. And kept backing all the way to the door. 'You're right. I don't. I'll get going. I've got some work, and—'

'Nic.' Her hands swept up to her face. 'Nic, no. I'm

sorry. I didn't mean that. I just…just snapped.' Shaking her head, she hurried towards him, eyes as huge as saucers.

'But we both know it's true.'

'No.' Light fingers touched his arm. 'Please… It's just… I've not been away, not even for one night, since they… left.' Her eyes brimmed with unshed tears. 'That's how it feels—like they just went on a trip and they'll come through that door any moment now, bursting to tell me all about their Alaskan cruise, and I need to be here in case—'

'It's okay, Charlotte.' He gently but firmly lifted her hand away. *I'm trying to understand.* Their Fiji fling suddenly seemed like a distant memory, and this girl wasn't the same girl he'd made love to every night for over two weeks. 'You should…get some rest. You didn't sleep much last night.'

'But you've just driven me all this way. Won't you stay for coffee at least?'

'It's best if I go. I'll see you soon.'

'Soon?' Her brow creased and her clouded grey eyes searched his face.

He knew it sounded vague. Damn, he was trying to get his head around all this. Because he had the urge to smooth that worry and hurt from her forehead, he stuck his hands in his pockets.

'Come for dinner.' She spoke as if she expected a refusal. 'I owe you a dinner, don't I? Tomorrow night.'

'I'll let you know.' He began walking down the hall towards the stairs.

Charlotte followed. 'Seven o'clock,' she said, her voice stronger as he turned to her at the front door. 'I'll do something special. Please, Nic?'

How could he resist those eyes? 'Okay. See you then.'

He drove with the window down and the wind screaming past his ear. He couldn't get the image of her standing in her parents' room out of his head. The pain, the grief still so bright and sharp. *Two years?*

She'd made the house a shrine to her family. From the little he knew of her life since her family's deaths, her decision to go to Fiji had been her best decision in those two years.

But now she was home would she build on her new experiences or slip into reverse and be satisfied existing on memories for the rest of her life? That wasn't living; it wasn't even close.

CHAPTER THIRTEEN

CHARLOTTE moped the rest of the day while she finished unpacking and restocked her groceries and tried to get on with things. The night was an endurance marathon, spent tossing and turning and regretting her defensiveness. Nic had been trying to help and she'd turned on him in the most unkind, hurtful, arrogant way possible. She'd accused him of not understanding *because of his background*.

And she'd realised it the moment the words were out of her mouth. She couldn't take them back. Could never take them back. She'd not meant it in a judgemental way, but how could he possibly understand family?

Through her bedroom window, she watched the night fade from grey to pink to day. Nic had been honest, his motivation purely based around concern *for her*, and the truth sliced like a blade. For a couple of weeks he'd made her forget, but coming home had been like taking a step backwards.

And he was right. Living here surrounded by reminders of the past was no way to live. The memories would always remain but she knew her family would be the first to tell her to move forward. They'd be cheering Nic on. It had taken getting away from everything familiar and comfortable—and Nic—to show her.

Her phone vibrated across her night stand. She was

only marginally disappointed when it was Suzette's voice and not Nic's.

'I'll be home this afternoon. I'll drop by around five,' Suzette told her. 'I've got some samples for the charity show ready for you to look at.'

'Ah, Nic's coming for dinner tonight.' If he hadn't changed his mind, that was.

'Oh? I thought it was over?'

Charlotte closed her eyes. 'Suz, have you got a few minutes? I need to talk…'

After the phone call, Charlotte got busy on the meal preparation. Fresh oysters, a lamb and potato hot pot and a sherry trifle. Easy cook, easy serve, would give her time to enjoy Nic's company and hopefully dispel the bad feeling they'd parted with.

She loved the cellar with its blend of rustic charm in the rough red bricks and the elegance of the eighteenth-century walnut dinner table and chairs. After setting the table with the best cutlery and china, she chose the wines for each course and set them aside.

Suzette was running late and she arrived with her sample pieces ten minutes before Nic was due.

Charlotte glanced at the clock. 'Can we bring them up to my room?' She did not want to face him surrounded by bridalwear.

'You are over Flynn, aren't you?' Suzette asked, a moment later, watching Charlotte carefully as she pulled a dress bag from her stash on the bed.

'Who? I've never been more over anyone or anything in my life.'

'Good. Still, I hope this won't upset you.' Suzette unzipped the bag. 'What do you think of this for the star attraction?' The hand-worked beading and cream pearls on the bodice winked like stars in the light. 'It would look amazing with your figure.'

Charlotte's heart clenched, but only for a moment. 'It's stunning,' she said slowly. 'But I'm no model. Anyway, I'll be busy making sure everything runs smoothly and people are buying.'

'And that's fine. I'd never ask you to do anything you're not comfortable with. I thought perhaps it might exorcise a demon or two.'

'Demons exorcised already. I feel better than I've felt in two years.'

'I can see that.' Suzette laid the garment on the bed. 'But be careful with this Nic guy, Charlie,' she warned, softly. 'I don't want to see you hurt again.'

Still hugging her arms, Charlotte looked away. 'I know, and I'll be careful. It's just…sometimes I think maybe, if he knew…'

'Knew what?'

That I love him and I can't imagine not being with him. She shook her head, made her voice brisk. 'Never mind. What's in this box?' She lifted a lid and pulled out a froth of tulle with diamanté tiara attached.

'From what you've told me, he sounds like great fling material but anything else…'

Charlotte wouldn't argue, not when her emotions were so close to spilling over. 'You're absolutely right. As usual. This is gorgeous.' She spun the headpiece around so that the tulle floated. 'Can I try it on?'

She didn't wait for an answer, putting it on her head and letting the tulle settle lightly over her face. A screen to hide the moisture that welled in her eyes.

Suzette adjusted the tiara from behind, then stepped back. 'I only finished it this afternoon—which is why I'm late—and I wanted to see how it looks from all sides in any case.' She twitched at the tulle. 'Good job, if I do say so myself.'

Charlotte turned and saw her misty reflection in the night-darkened window. And for just a heartbeat out of time, she dreamed the impossible dream.

Nic arrived a few moments early. He'd seen a car ahead as he turned into the drive and had killed the lights and stopped. A tall, leggy blonde in the highest heels he'd ever seen had got out with a load of stuff; the two women had hugged then gone inside. Suzette?

They probably had loads to discuss. He had a feeling he was about to feel his ears burning. He stared up at the house where light spilled from an upstairs window.

He inched the car forward and parked behind the woman's SUV as Charlotte appeared in the window. Something white and filmy and nuptial covered her dark hair. She fluffed it out, obviously watching herself in the glass. *That* was precisely why he and Charlotte wouldn't work long term.

But his gut tightened nevertheless. And if he sat here much longer he might see more than he was supposed to. Definitely more than he wanted to. Charlotte was expecting him ten minutes ago. How would it look if they came outside and found him sitting in his car like a Peeping Tom?

Grabbing the armful of daffodils, he walked to the door and rang the bell.

A moment later, the door opened and the blonde smiled at him. 'Hi. You must be Nic. I'm Suzette.'

'Hi, Suzette.'

She motioned him inside. 'Charlotte'll be down in a moment. Gorgeous flowers; she'll love them.'

'I've caught her at a bad time.'

'Not at all. It's me who's in the way. I just dropped by to leave a few things here for the show.'

He shifted uncomfortably and ran a hand inside the neck of his jumper. He knew when he was being sized up for a wedding suit. Or possibly a coffin if he did anything to hurt Charlotte, because something in Suzette's eyes advised him to proceed with caution. 'You're a successful designer, I hear.'

She smiled. 'I like to think so.'

'What do you think of Charlotte's designs?'

'She's shown you?' Then she laughed lightly, blue eyes twinkling. 'I guess she has. I love them. I'm hoping she'll let us use some of her pieces at the show.'

'Good. Because I think she could make a go of it, if she decided to get serious.'

'I totally agree. We'll have to join forces and talk her into it.'

Her smile was friendly enough but he could tell it came with a warning that if he broke rank she'd crush him with her stilettoed heel.

She glanced over her shoulder. 'Here she comes now.'

Charlotte descended the stairs, wearing a fluffy jumper the colour of melted butter and black leggings that showcased her legs.

'I told you that colour suited you years ago,' Suzette said as she swept out. 'Nice to meet you, Nic.'

'Yeah.' He didn't notice her leave. He was too busy looking at the woman he'd come to see. 'New jumper?'

'I decided I needed something that reminds me of sunshine. Maybe it'll hurry spring along.'

'In that case, I chose well.' He handed her the matching flowers, then bent forward to kiss her lips.

'They're gorgeous. Thank you.' She smiled up at him

but there was an awareness of yesterday's scene in her soft grey eyes.

'I'll just get some water… Come through.'

The warm and enticing aroma of herbs and lamb filled the hall as he followed her to the kitchen. She arranged the daffodils in a vase, then picked it up. 'This way. Everything's ready.'

She led him down a narrow flight of stairs off the kitchen and his pulse picked up its pace as the walls narrowed and leaned towards him. He knew it was only his perception.

'The cellar's one of my favourite places,' she said as they descended. 'It's intimate without being confining.'

And to some extent she was right, thank God. If the ceiling weren't quite so low, it'd be even better. Haunting classical guitar drifted through hidden speakers, a crystal chandelier tossed rainbows over a long table set for two at one end. There were delicate pink wine glasses and polished silver.

How was this for a turn-around—Nic being romanced by a woman? A woman he cared deeply about. More than cared about… The knowledge and his instant refusal to accept that knowledge threw him off balance for a moment. For once in his adult life he wasn't the one in control. In more ways than one.

'Do you mind leaving the door open?' He scratched at the itch around his neck. 'I'm feeling a little warm.'

'Of course.' She moved to the table as she spoke. 'But it's always a constant temperature down here. I'm sure you'll be okay.'

She positioned the daffodils in the centre next to an ornate silver candelabrum, then pressed her palms together. 'Perfect.' She smiled at him, the chandelier's lights sparkling in her eyes like stars.

He smiled back. 'How could it not be? You went to all this trouble for me.'

'Nothing's too much trouble for you.'

Careful, Nic. 'This is great,' he said to the room in general, wandering over to study what looked to his inexperienced eye to be an original and highly prized piece of Australian art. 'Where's the wine? Shouldn't a cellar have wine?'

'Through there.' She gestured to a slim archway almost obscured by a wrought-iron grille. 'I'll show you later. For now, have a seat,' she said, withdrawing a plate of oysters au naturel and a bottle from a bar fridge. 'Wine?'

'Allow me—'

She whisked it out of his reach. 'I'm the hostess—I'm quite capable of pouring wine. We'll start with a chardonnay.' She paused, the bottle in mid-air. 'If you'd like?'

He sat where she'd indicated. 'I'm in your capable hands.'

She shot him a smouldering look. 'Let's just eat first. This is one of our best.' She poured the amber liquid, then sat down herself and raised her glass. 'I hope you like it. It has a tropical fruit flavour I think you'll appreciate and pairs up well with seafood.'

'To good wine.' There was the tinkle of delicate glass on glass as he touched his flute to hers.

She nodded. 'And hopefully good food.'

'Nice.' He savoured its crisp and sweet taste on his tongue a moment, then scooped up an oyster. 'You grow any other varieties?'

'We're mainly into Shiraz, which the Barossa's famous for. Three Cockatoos Winery has won barrelfuls of awards over the years. We'll try some with our main…' She trailed off, her eyes clouded and staring into space.

'What's wrong?'

'I forgot the winery's no longer a part of my life.'

He stretched a hand to hers across the table. 'Tell me about it. The winery, your family.'

With apparent effort she turned her focus on him. 'My mother's ancestors were among the first German settlers in the nineteenth century. My father's three times great grandfather migrated from France during the gold rush, made his fortune, then came to the Barossa and grew grapes. The Dumonts have always been here. And I sold them out.' Her voice dropped to a near whisper.

'No.' He turned her hand over and caressed her palm with his thumb and stared into her troubled eyes. 'You have a heritage you can be proud of no matter who owns the winery now.'

Her gaze clouded further and he knew she was thinking about his manifestly vast *lack* of background and heritage because hadn't she made that quite clear yesterday? The princess and the boy from the back streets? He withdrew his hand.

'Nic. About yesterday. I—'

'Don't. There's no need.'

'But there is, I—'

The world plunged into darkness. Black. Totally, blindingly, unfathomably black. Nic closed his eyes so he couldn't see it while his mind shut down and shrivelled into survival mode. *Breathe. Breathe. Breathe.* He concentrated only on reciting the word in his head and tried unsuccessfully to visualise a cool lake. All he could see were pin spots dancing on his eyelids.

'That damn cellar fuse must have blown again,' he heard her say through the thickening air that pressed in around him.

He didn't even attempt to speak. To do so would make him appear an idiot and, besides, his throat had closed over.

He felt the vibrations as she shuffled and bumped her way along the edge of the table towards him. A hand brushed his arm. 'Stay put. I'll be back in a jiff.'

Sweat broke out on his brow, his back. His worst nightmare. She was going to leave him here alone underground in the dark. *Scaredy cat, scaredy cat, scared of the dark.* Old pleas, old taunts. *Leering faces circling him, closer, closer till he couldn't breathe. Holding his schoolbag like a trophy, too high for a young boy to reach. Waving a blindfold in front of his eyes. Let's teach him a lesson he won't forget.*

'Stop!' He hadn't realised he'd spoken his mantra aloud until he felt her jolt. 'You'll trip; I'll come too.' He managed by sheer terrifying necessity to get the words past his quivering tonsils.

'I'm okay,' she said cheerfully. 'I know my way around, you don't.'

'I insist,' he gritted out, jerking off the chair. It tipped over with a clatter of splintering wood. *Antique wood.* He took a step, stumbled over it.

'Hey.' She laughed lightly. 'I should be the one helping you.'

He felt her hand and clutched at it like a damn lifeline. 'Fine. I'm fine.'

'No, you're not.' A pause. 'You're trembling…' Another pause—concerned and amazed.

She knew.

'Come on,' she said softly and led him to the stairs. 'Fifteen steps; count them.'

It gave him something to concentrate on as he felt his way, the rough bricks catching on his jumper, his shoes scudding against the stairs.

Finally. Fresh air was a cool relief on his sweat-soaked brow and he could make out the shape of the fridge, the old sideboard with its stained-glass frontage and Charlotte's eyes glinting in the kitchen's dimness. She flicked a switch and he blinked in the flood of light and pulled his hand out of her grasp.

'What just went on down there, Nic?' she asked quietly, her gaze searching his.

He scrubbed his hands over his jaw. 'What are you talking about?' He backed away on legs that felt like reeds in a wind. 'I'll be outside. I forgot something in the car.'

'Nic.' She reached for him, caught hold of his arms and stepped in front, barring his way. 'You have a fear of confined spaces?'

'Don't be ridiculous.'

'*I'm* not being ridiculous.' Her hold tightened. 'Typical man—your worst fear is admitting that you *have* a fear. Fear isn't weakness, and I want to help.'

He stood stiffly, his jaw clenched. 'If you want to help, you can terminate this conversation.'

Her eyes were resolute and full of compassion. 'My nurturing side won't let me.'

'I don't need nurturing, for God's sake.' He flicked his gaze to the ceiling, away from her soft grey eyes that seemed to plumb the depths of his soul.

'Okay, not nurturing, then. I'm talking support. Even the toughest guy needs support now and then. The trick is acknowledging and accepting it.'

He wouldn't know how. He'd been on his own so long he'd learned to live without it. He'd forgotten how to lean on another, but suddenly he yearned, desperately, to bury his head at Charlotte's breast and draw on her comfort. Worse, he was afraid if he did, he'd never let go.

Instead, he played to one of his key strengths and dropped his voice to a seductive murmur he was far from feeling. 'Support's not what I need from you, babe.'

Running his hands over the sides of her breasts to the slim curve of her waist, he leaned in to kiss her but she pushed him away hard and her eyes flashed with impatience.

'So I'm good enough to have sex with but not good enough to lean on and confide in and be *someone who matters.*'

He cursed himself when he recognised it wasn't only impatience he saw, there was hurt too. 'Damn it, Charlotte, that's n—'

'When you love someone you want to help that person any way you can. Why can't you see that? Why *won't* you see that?'

That shocked both of them into silence. *Love.* Such an overrated, overused word. But why did that single word sound so right—so complete, so *perfect*— coming from Charlotte's lips? Why did it wrap around his heart so tight he wondered how it didn't shatter into a million pieces?

He beat it down. An illusion was what it was. What it all was. And he didn't need it. He was happy with his life. Free and easy and unencumbered. And no self-respecting woman needed a man who cracked like a faulty tower every time there was a mini power failure.

He paced away, using the kitchen table as a barrier between them. 'I travel solo, Charlotte. You understood right from the start.'

'So now I'm a threat to you and your precious independence.'

'A holiday romance was all I offered and what you agreed to. I've never been anything but honest with you.'

'Honest,' she said slowly and he could hear the burn of frustration and anger. 'Is that what you're being? What about that little performance on the balcony? You'd prefer to freeze your arse off than talk to me. And tonight… Your problem's a common one and yet you deny—'

'You don't know jack.' He turned to her, his own frustration and impotence at boiling point. 'And I don't need you psychoanalysing me.'

'Is that what you call it?' Her eyes clashed with his. He could almost hear the swords cross. 'It's so much more than that, Nic, but you're not ready or willing to share, and I'm sorry for you.'

She sighed. Not an audible sigh, but one that passed from her heart to his and shadowed the world grey.

'I never meant to—'

'Leave. I don't want to hear it. I've been shut out once too often. I refuse to be shut out any more. People I love always leave—why should you be any different?'

'Charlotte…' He couldn't find the words. Why couldn't he find the right words?

'After all,' she continued, on a roll now, 'as you just stated very clearly, it was never anything more than a holiday fling.'

The way she said it, as if it were the most casual of affairs when deep down he knew it wasn't, made him want to yell something. But what? *I love you too and it might have started as a fling and now it's more but it can never work.*

'Go.'

'Okay. Calm down. Tomorrow we'll—'

She threw up a hand. 'Don't come back, Nic. I don't want you here. It's over.'

It took him a skipped heartbeat to process her meaning, then the hot taste of panic skewered up his throat. He grasped for a reason to make her change her mind. 'The benefit; you'll need some support.'

'Support?' Her laugh was harsh, scraping at his soul. 'Oh, you're a fine one to talk of support.' She curled her hands into fists at her sides. 'I planned it because I wanted to give something back to Kas and the kids. I never intended you to be involved—you invited yourself. Well, I'm uninviting you.' She rapped a fist once on the table. 'I don't *need* your support, the way you don't *need* mine, so we're square.'

He acknowledged that with a tilt of his head. 'If that's how you want it.'

'It is.'

She glared at him, eyes dry now but he knew there'd be tears soon enough. It was kinder to finish it quickly and cleanly and be done. Over. *Don't give her a reason to think there's more.*

He rubbed at the raw throbbing place over his heart, forced a smile and played his last card. 'Goodbye, Charlotte. It's been fun. Look me up if you ever get to Fiji again.' He waved a disparaging hand in the air. 'That is if you can bring yourself to leave this mausoleum.'

CHAPTER FOURTEEN

'THAT'S the last of it.'

Charlotte dipped her thumbs into the back pockets of her jeans and watched the final box of memories being loaded into the truck. It had taken two weeks of tears and sleeplessness to sort through her family's stuff, decide what to keep and what to toss.

'You okay?' Suzette asked beside her as they watched the truck's doors close.

'I will be.' Between clearing out the house and organising the fashion show she'd had no time for dilly-dallying and broken hearts. She'd made decisions on the spot; she'd live with her choices.

At least the busyness helped keep her mind off Nic, if only for short bursts. The nights were the worst; dreams and heartache and memories. How many times had she picked up the phone to call him and say she'd changed her mind, then reminded herself he'd been the one insisting it was temporary? It had just ended sooner than she'd thought. The big surprise was that she'd done the ending.

Suzette slung an arm around her shoulders as the vehicle trundled away. 'Let's take a coffee break before that antique dealer arrives with his quotes.'

'Good idea.' Charlotte leaned into her as they walked inside to the noise of hammering and drills. In the formal lounge a guy was installing a monitoring system to keep a watchful eye when she opened the room to the public. She still had to decide which of the antiques to sell and which to keep, and that process would require more consideration. Because what stayed would be a key component of her new plans for this place.

On their way through the kitchen they passed a couple of tradesmen installing her big new oven. 'This is the right decision.'

'Yes, it *so* is. I guess I have to be grateful to that Nic guy for something,' Suzette murmured the moment they were past and out of earshot. 'If nothing else, he forced you to see what I've been trying to get you to see for two years.'

The mention of his name was like a fist at her breastbone. 'We may be over, but he's still the best thing that ever happened to me.'

Suzette stopped and looked at her deep and direct, eyes full of understanding and sympathy. 'You still love him.'

'Yes.' And that reality was a raw and open wound. 'It'll take time but I'll get through it.'

'He hurt you.'

'Because I let him, Suz. It wasn't his fault—he never made a secret of what he wanted—and I knew he had that power but I jumped right in regardless. Now I'm living with the consequences.'

She stopped at the entrance to the atrium her father had had erected the year before he'd died. The pungent smell of rich damp earth greeted them. Sunshine poured in, throwing shards of rose and emerald onto the luxurious greenery through two intricately stained-glass panels. The rest of the atrium was clear glass and allowed plenty of natural light. Sliding floor-to-ceiling windows could be opened on a fine day to bring the fragrance of the herb garden inside.

The worst had happened. It could only get better from

hereon in. But something good had come out of the bad too. Nic had given her affirmation as a woman. She'd bloomed like the flowering vine that climbed the atrium's walls because Nic had shown her how. She no longer wanted to blend into the background; she wanted to shine like the sun glinting on the glass.

'I love this room.' Smiling for what felt like the first time in weeks, she nodded to where a stack of new café chairs towered beside half a dozen small tables. There were glass display shelves and clothing racks against the wall. 'And I'm going to turn it into my dream.'

Nic gazed over the white-capped ocean. Sea mist blurred the horizon today, whipped by a strong wind. *The colour of Charlotte's eyes.* For the third time in as many minutes his hand hovered over his phone. Tonight was Charlotte's big night. He should ring, let her know he was thinking of her and wish her luck.

But she'd told him it was over. The last thing he wanted to do was reopen fresh wounds. He should have gone back to Fiji as he'd intended, but he'd not been able to put that stamp of finality on their relationship.

'Why not?' he asked the ceiling for the millionth time. She'd seemed so sure that was what she wanted on that last night when she told him it was over. And wasn't it what he wanted too? It had just happened too damn soon.

Tossing his phone across the desk, he brought his manuscript up on screen. Two solid weeks of work and he'd almost finished, but he couldn't see the end.

Reena is imprisoned in the Sphere of Darkness. Onyx flies to the rescue on his trusted dragon, Grodinor. Happy ever after...

But how?

He drummed his fingers on his thighs. If his own life

were one of his games how would he play it? Charlotte, his real-life heroine. Beautiful. Loving and fun to be with. Unique—her understated dress code, her empathy for others, her ability to pull a fundraiser together at short notice. And trapped as surely as Reena, unable and unwilling to let go of her past.

But was Nic Russo hero material? Hardly. Was he any different to her? Suddenly, like Charlotte, he realised he was trapped in a hole of his own making, unable to unlock his fears and share them with someone who cared, someone who could help him to heal. *Someone who loved him.*

He spun his chair towards the ocean view but he wasn't seeing it. The last time with Charlotte played before his eyes like an old movie. There was something very wrong with that scene...

But what?

Had he thought himself free? Was that truly what he wanted or was it a barrier he'd erected to keep people at a distance, something to hide the deep down longing to connect with another? To trust and belong. To be accepted for his faults and failings.

He not only feared confined spaces, he was afraid of not being good enough.

He was afraid of rejection.

Whoa... He scrubbed his hands over his four-day stubble and let the dust of this new realisation settle. He was the independent playboy, the charmer, superficial, because that kid from the back streets was still afraid of being excluded. An outsider looking in, telling himself he didn't want to belong anyway.

He'd found solace in his safe world of make-believe. But that world was no longer enough. It was a prison, a way of avoiding reality, as surely as Charlotte's family home was for her.

He needed the real world, with a real woman. Charlotte. And if he didn't lay his fears and faults on the table, whether he was accepted with them or not, he'd never experience the freedom he really craved. And faults and all, he'd never find the love he knew he could find with Charlotte. If she'd have him back. *Real* love, a *real* life, not some fantasy world to hide away in.

His chair rolled backwards across the boards as he shot up, checking his watch on his way to the bathroom. There was still time…

'Good evening, ladies and gentlemen.' Charlotte smiled at the audience and waited for the crowd to hush. To look at *her*. The press was there at her invitation. Her parents' friends. New faces and old. Was she really standing up here in front of all these people? Her hand trembled on the microphone but she took a deep steadying breath.

'Thank you for coming and for your support for this worthy cause. As some of you know, I was recently in Fiji and had the opportunity to visit a local school.' She scanned the crowd but there was no sign of the man she'd foolishly hoped might be there. 'I'd like to acknowledge a man who not only makes generous monetary donations, but gives his time and expertise every week to support those students who play and learn under less privileged circumstances than our children here in Australia. His name's Nic Russo. Nic's kind and generous and…' her voice faltered '…and his work's the inspiration for tonight's show.' Pinning her smile back in place, she said, 'I hope you'll all dig deep tonight and purchase some of Suzette's stunning pieces that you'll see this evening.'

Nic arrived at the entrance as Charlotte finished her introduction and what he saw stole his breath—and his heart—clean away. Charlotte, *his* Charlotte, in fire-engine red. A slinky shimmering low-cut gown that clung to every curve. A poised and confident woman who'd do any damn politician proud.

And she'd paid *Nic* tribute. It made him humble and proud and very, very grateful she'd come into his life and changed it for ever.

As she turned to leave the runway he sucked in a breath. The full-length gown was backless, right down to the dip in her spine. Her shoes, glittering crimson stilettos, peeked from beneath the hem as she walked away and disappeared behind the screen.

He couldn't wait to talk to her, to touch her again and tell her... He had so much to tell her, but that would have to wait. Not wanting to distract her, he spotted a vacant seat near the back.

Fashion shows weren't his thing, especially when all he could think was, when would it finish? His attention was ostensibly on the models parading some way-out bridal and formal designs, but his mind was on the woman he'd not even glimpsed since that initial speech on his arrival.

'And now for some scintillating, sexy lingerie,' he heard the announcer say with a grin in her voice, and perked up. 'Nothing too risqué; *those* are available for your personal perusal in your catalogue.'

Models started coming out wearing what he recognised as Charlotte's work, but he wasn't prepared for the finale— the long-legged brunette gliding along the runway in a white gauze number over flamingo-pink bra and panties.

Charlotte.

He could only think...*hot*.

Too soon, she disappeared behind the screen but in no time at all she was back on the runway again wearing that fabulous red gown.

He started making his way through the audience as the announcer handed Charlotte the microphone.

'Thank you, ladies and gentlemen,' she said, her face flushed, her eyes sparkling. 'That's all and goodnight. Oh, don't forget to buy a raffle ticket or ten before you leave.' She pointed to a couple of the models starting to circulate amongst the crowd. 'The prize is a weekend getaway at a mystery location.' She handed the microphone back and began descending the steps.

Not bothering with the stairs, Nic hauled himself onto the runway and took the microphone from the surprised announcer. 'Ladies and gentlemen, before you leave...'

The audience murmured and looked at him expectantly. He only had eyes for one member of that audience and she was frozen to the carpet. Her smile had vanished; the pretty flush had leached away. He smiled encouragement at her before turning to the audience once more. 'Good evening. My name's Nic Russo.'

More shuffles and murmurs. Maybe it was a mistake to muscle in on Charlotte's event, but it wasn't his biggest mistake. His biggest mistake had been letting her walk out of his life.

'I'd like a chance to say a few words about Charlotte. I met her a month ago in Fiji. No, that's not quite correct—I met her at Tullamarine airport.' He looked down into her eyes. 'How would I describe Charlotte Dumont? She's capable. She organised this event in two short weeks. She's creative. You saw her designs up here tonight. I don't know about you, but I'll be purchasing a few pieces for my special woman, if not the entire collection, so you'd better be quick if you don't want to miss out.

'But most of all, she cares. She saw a need and made it a priority and that's why we're here tonight.' *She's the most amazing woman I've ever met. She's the woman I love.* 'So please, everyone, help her out, and help give some kids in Fiji a fantastic environment to play and learn in because that's where the money raised tonight will go.'

As he handed the microphone back Nic saw the flash of red disappear through a rear door. His heart jumped into his mouth and he followed.

Light bulbs flashed and reporters rushed him at the door. 'Does Dom Silverman have something to say?' someone asked.

Nic stopped short. Nodded. 'I'll give you guys some time to ask questions later, but can you do me a favour and disappear for now?' He shot them a grin. 'I have something important to tell Ms Dumont. In private.'

Heedless of the cold air on her bare arms and back and the glitter of flashbulbs, Charlotte fled down the wide steps and onto the lawns that lined the river. Her heart was numb with shock and a lot more.

The city's lights reflected on the water, the fountain's spray speared high into the sky, captured in changing colours of green, pink, purple, yellow.

Nic was still here. He'd come and he'd paid her the highest of compliments. He'd told the entire audience he intended purchasing her collection for his 'special woman'. He'd looked at her when he'd said it.

Shivering, she rubbed her arms and wished she'd grabbed her jacket, but she'd been in too much of a rush to avoid Nic. A couple strolled hand in hand along the bank, obviously in love.

Yes, she loved Nic, she always would and once upon a time that couple might have been them, but she'd told him no. She was strong enough to tell him no again.

She'd started a new life, one that didn't include broken hearts and dreams that didn't come true and men who weren't prepared to give everything, to share everything. Halfway was *not* enough.

She clenched her fists against her sides, summoning anger and indignation to crush the pain she'd worked so hard to be rid of. How dared he appear at her special event after two weeks of silence, smiling at her in that intimate way, arrogantly speaking of Tullamarine airport *as if nothing had changed*?

She knew he was coming for her long before he reached her. It was as if she had inbuilt radar where Nic was concerned.

'Charlotte.'

She didn't turn around. 'Hi, Nic.'

'You were sensational tonight. Congratulations.'

'Thanks.' He still hadn't touched her and, despite herself, her body yearned.

'The evening was a great success by the looks of things.'

'I hope it helps.' They were talking like two acquaintances discussing an opera performance. Two strangers who'd run out of conversation. She studied the ground as if she might find the right words to say written on the grass.

'This may not be the lake I imagined,' Nic began. 'And maybe the stars are already out, or maybe those reflections on the water are fallen stars—a bit like me. Because since we parted that's how I feel. Like I'm at the bottom of that dark murky River Torrens.'

She crossed her arms, tightened her fingers above her elbows, so tight she could feel her nails bite into the flesh. 'Perhaps you need to think about how you got there and find a way out.'

One warm finger touched the back of her neck. Gently, as if she might splinter into a million pieces. And she was very afraid it might be true.

'Where are your pearls?'

'I don't need them to remember my mother any more. She's in my heart.' *Like you.* 'I've made some changes in my life, Nic.'

'I can see that,' he murmured, his voice like velvet, and she knew he was looking at her dress. 'Told you you'd look hot in red.'

She heard the shifting of fabric and then his coat was over her shoulders, smelling warm and familiar.

His arms came around her. 'I hope there's room in your changed life for me, Charlotte, because I can't stand not being with you. Because, you see, sweetheart, I love you too.'

Tears sprang to her eyes, blurring the water's reflections, and she shook her head. 'When people love each other they talk. Flynn didn't talk to me. I never knew what he was thinking, that he was interested in politics, even whether I came up to scratch as a future politician's wife. He never gave me a chance to change and then he left.'

Nic pulled her back against him so he could feel her body tucked tight into his. Breathed in her signature perfume. 'I'm glad he did. Because now you're mine.'

She stiffened and he felt her withdrawal and a knife of panic sliced through him.

'I won't be shut out, Nic.'

'Then how about this… My name's Nic Russo, I love you and I'm also a claustrophobic. Which means I dissolve into a quivering mess in confined spaces. I'd like to talk about it with you if you'll listen.' The silence was like a dark night with no end. 'Will you listen to me, Charlotte? Will you hear my story and hold me while I tell you? Because the darkness in your cellar's nothing compared to the darkness inside me right now.'

Her silence was the longest silence he'd ever known but then she nodded slowly. 'I will.'

She turned in his arms, and stroked back the hair from his temples with fingers that were strong yet tender. Her eyes were the soft mist of the ocean and filled with compassion and love and understanding. 'You know I will.'

He was barely aware of the glitter from half a dozen paparazzi cameras. 'Then how about we get out of here?'

She jutted her chin at something over his shoulder. 'I suppose we'd better give those guys something to write about first.'

'You mean like this?' He kissed her the way she deserved to be kissed; slowly and thoroughly.

When he finally let her go, she shook her head, but her eyes were dancing. 'I meant give them a story. We've already done the public kiss. *Honey Pie.*'

'Ah, so we have,' he murmured. 'So are you up for it? For them?'

Taking his hand, she began walking up the grass towards the press, his coat swinging from her shoulders. 'You better believe it.'

He laid her on his bed and in the silvery light of a half moon, with fused gazes and hearts open and willing, they silently undressed each other. Skin on skin, nothing between them. With every touch a murmur, every breath a wish, every heartbeat, joy. They made love slowly, deeply, truly and when they'd assuaged the physical needs, they turned to each other. Only then did they talk.

'I had a mother but I raised myself,' Nic began, staring at the ceiling. He told her about his waitress poker-addicted mother and how he was often left alone as it grew dark and how his runaway imagination used to get the better of him.

'Nic, I'm so sorry.'

'It gets worse,' he went on, still unable to look at her, the words tumbling out now in the relief of sharing and his trust in Charlotte that he'd not be ridiculed. 'The school was in a rough neighbourhood. The local bullies would wait for me in the park on the way home. Sometimes they'd hold me down, kick the crap out of me and laugh about it the next day in the school yard.'

Her love and her shock were obvious in her quiet voice. 'Why didn't you tell someone?'

'I was too damn scared. But one day I did—I told my teacher. A big mistake on my part because a few days later they tied me up, blindfolded me and left me in a Dumpster at the back of some shops.'

'Oh my God, Nic...'

'I was there over twenty-four hours before the kids decided to own up and the police found me.'

The lack of emotion in his voice, as if it was just another injustice in a world full of injustices, squeezed Charlotte's heart. She touched his hair, his face, his lips, wishing he'd look at her. No wonder he was so scarred. 'That's why you didn't let me blindfold you...'

'I had a lot of time to think in there.' His tone was tinged with an odd humour. 'I found I was pretty good at making up stories of how I'd escape and discovering weird and wonderful ways to get my revenge.'

'And did you get your revenge?'

At last he looked at her. Smiled at her in the darkness. 'I got that when I made my first million from those stories of vengeance and justice and fantasy I'd dreamed up. I used them in my games.'

She smiled back. 'What happened after you were found?'

'Mum changed jobs, we moved to a new flat in a better area and things improved. But I've been claustrophobic ever since.'

'And you've not had professional counselling?'

'No. But I'm ready now. I've learnt something else in

the last couple of weeks.' He took her hand, pressed it over his heart where she could feel it beating strong and steady. 'My greatest fear's putting myself and my love for you on the line and having you not want it.'

'Of course I want it.' She covered his face with butterfly kisses. 'I want it all. It was you not letting me in that I couldn't deal with. It was like you'd already left and it hurt as deeply as when my family died and I didn't want that pain in my life again.'

His eyes were dark and filled with determination and love. 'No more pain, sweetheart. When bad things happen, as they inevitably do in life, we'll deal with it together.'

Then he spent the next little while showing her how exactly it was going to be.

Finally, pushing up to a sitting position against the bed head, he gathered her against his chest. 'Now it's your turn to fill me in on your plans.'

'My plans may have just changed.'

He stroked her hair. 'Tell me anyway.'

'I decided to use part of the house to try selling my lingerie. I'm closing off some rooms for private use and opening up the rest to the public to sell off the family heirlooms. People can come and taste Three Cockatoos wine and home-made nibbles and browse clothing and antiques at the same time.'

'But you sold the winery, sweetheart...' he murmured.

'Yes, but their daughter, Ella, is interested in my idea. She's going to come on board and help on a trial basis first. If it works out, I can put her in as a manager and it'll give me time to do other things.'

'Sounds like success all round.'

'The only problem now is the long-distance relationship,' she said.

'There's not going to be any long-distance relationship.

If Ella works out, she can take over when we go to Fiji.
I can work anywhere. We'll figure it out as we go along.
The important thing is that we figure it out side by side.
Together.'

And the future was suddenly rosy and filled with love
and hope.

EPILOGUE

Three months later.

THE beach at sunset was officially perfect. The sand was
pungent with the fresh scent of recent rain and strewn
with petals, the air moist and warm, the sky a burnished
gold shot with purple. Flickering kerosene torches surrounded the intimate circle of friends who'd gathered for
the ceremony.

The only thing missing from the perfect scene was a
perfect bride.

The anxious groom wore white; white trousers and a
loose white Island shirt—as requested. His feet were bare.
Also requested.

Nic held his breath as the faint sounds of banjos and
ukuleles playing something dreamy and appropriate for the
moment grew closer, heralding the bride's arrival.

And then, suddenly, there she was. His heroine. His
Charlotte. For a moment his eyes blurred, because his life,
his love, his whole world, was approaching him, her eyes
the colour of sea mist and locked on his, her smile radiant.

For once in his life, he didn't mind traditionally conservative. Wearing one of Suzette's creations, she looked
like a princess in a white beaded gown that flowed to
her bare feet. She'd threaded crimson flowers through her

long hair; two heavy garlands of those same flowers hung around her neck.

He let out that breath on a slow sigh of relief, and smiled back. It seemed his story was to have a happy ending after all.

'Hi, there, you,' she whispered, and lifted one of the garlands she was wearing and placed it around his neck.

'Welcome, friends.' The celebrant, a friend of Suzette's, smiled at the group. 'We're here on this glorious tropical evening to make it official between these two people…'

'So here we are.' Charlotte linked her hands around Nic's neck later as they danced—or, rather, swayed—across the makeshift dance floor under the stars to the surprise and delight of Vaka Malua's guests.

'Yep. Here we are.' He bent to place a lingering kiss on her lips. 'Did you ever think otherwise?'

'There was a time…'

'Nah. It was always a foregone conclusion.' He leaned closer, nuzzling her neck. 'I was yours from the first moment you stood in front of me in the queue at Tullamarine. And my instincts are always spot on.'

'I've missed you,' she murmured. 'I never knew a week could take so long.'

'Hmm,' he agreed, smoothing his hands over her back and sending delicious tingles all through her body.

She had stayed on in Adelaide a week longer than Nic to ensure a smooth transition for Old and New, the only place she knew that offered lingerie and antiques over a choice of wine or coffee.

Never again—from now on it was always going to be the two of them. And it was official. She wiggled the fingers on her left hand to admire her newest sparkle.

'Everything under control with the new place?'

'Ella's going to make a fine manager.' She caught sight of Suzette and Tenika grinning at her and gave them a cheeky finger wave. 'She spoke to me this morning; she's already sold three sets of lingerie and a chest of drawers.'

'Hmm,' he murmured, the rough velvet rumble hot against her ear. 'Speaking of lingerie, do you reckon this party can carry on without us? I can't wait to see what surprises you've got in store for me tonight.'

'I can't wait to see what surprises you've got for me either.' She grinned up at him, loving their sexy banter and innuendo. Loving the way they brought out the best in each other. Then she took his hand and began leading him away. 'Come on, I'll show you.'

* * * * *

A sneaky peek at next month...

MODERN™

INTERNATIONAL AFFAIRS, SEDUCTION & PASSION GUARANTEED

My wish list for next month's titles...

In stores from 16th November 2012:

☐ A Ring to Secure His Heir — Lynne Graham

☐ Woman in a Sheikh's World — Sarah Morgan

☐ At His Majesty's Request — Maisey Yates

☐ The Ruthless Caleb Wilde — Sandra Marton

In stores from 7th December 2012:

☐ What His Money Can't Hide — Maggie Cox

☐ At Dante's Service — Chantelle Shaw

☐ Breaking the Greek's Rules — Anne McAllister

☐ The Price of Success — Maya Blake

☐ The Man From her Wayward Past — Susan Stephens

Available at WHSmith, Tesco, Asda, Eason, Amazon and Apple

Just can't wait?

Visit us Online

You can buy our books online a month before they hit the shops! **www.millsandboon.co.uk**

1112/01

Special Offers

Every month we put together collections and longer reads written by your favourite authors.

Here are some of next month's highlights— and don't miss our fabulous discount online!

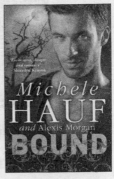

On sale 16th November

On sale 16th November

On sale 7th December

Save 20%
on all Special Releases

MILLS & BOON® Book Club

2 Free Books!

Get your free books now at
www.millsandboon.co.uk/freebookoffer

Or fill in the form below and post it back to us

THE MILLS & BOON® BOOK CLUB™—HERE'S HOW IT WORKS: Accepting your free books places you under no obligation to buy anything. You may keep the books and return the despatch note marked 'Cancel'. If we do not hear from you, about a month later we'll send you 4 brand-new stories from the Modern™ series priced at £3.49* each. There is no extra charge for post and packaging. You may cancel at any time, otherwise we will send you 4 stories a month which you may purchase or return to us—the choice is yours. *Terms and prices subject to change without notice. Offer valid in UK only. Applicants must be 18 or over. Offer expires 31st January 2013. **For full terms and conditions, please go to www.millsandboon.co.uk/freebookoffer**

Mrs/Miss/Ms/Mr (please circle) _____

First Name _____

Surname _____

Address _____

_____

_____ Postcode _____

E-mail _____

Send this completed page to: Mills & Boon Book Club, Free Book Offer, FREEPOST NAT 10298, Richmond, Surrey, TW9 1BR

Find out more at
www.millsandboon.co.uk/freebookoffer

Visit us Online

0712/P2YEA

Have Your Say

You've just finished your book.
So what did you think?

We'd love to hear your thoughts on our
'Have your say' online panel
www.millsandboon.co.uk/haveyoursay

- 🌹 Easy to use
- 🌹 Short questionnaire
- 🌹 Chance to win Mills & Boon® goodies